THE
Prophet's Kid

KidWitness Tales

KiDWiTNESS
T·A·L·E·S

THE
Prophet's Kid

JIM WARE

BETHANYHOUSE

MINNEAPOLIS, MINNESOTA

A Focus on the Family book.
Published by Bethany House Publishers
A Ministry of Bethany Fellowship International
11400 Hampshire Avenue South
Bloomington, Minnesota 55438
www.bethanyhouse.com

Printed in the United States of America by
Bethany Press International, Bloomington, Minnesota 55438

Library of Congress Cataloging-in-Publication Data
Ware, Jim.
    The prophet's kid / by Jim Ware.
        p.   cm. — (KidWitness tales)
"A Focus on the Family book."
Summary: Ezra and his friends, which include the son of the prophet Isaiah and the son of King Ahaz, learn firsthand the terrible consequences of forsaking the Lord and following false gods.
    ISBN 1-56179-965-3
    1. Jews—History—To 586 B.C.—Juvenile fiction. [1. Jews—History—To 586 B.C.—Fiction. 2. Bible. O.T.—History of Biblical events—Fiction. 3. Jerusalem—History—Fiction.] I. Title. II. Series.
    PZ7.W219 Pr   2001
    [Fic]—dc21   2001001272

1 2 3 4 5 6 7 8 9 10 11 12 13 14 15 / 08 07 06 05 04 03 02 01

For Al, Lissa, John, and Kathy,

who helped make it happen

JIM WARE is a graduate of Fuller Theological Seminary. He and his wife, Joni, have six kids—Alison, Megan, Bridget, Ian, Brittany, and Callum. Just for fun, Jim plays the guitar and the hammered dulcimer.

In the great hall of Ahaz the King all was festive and bright. Cups clattered. The voices of the guests echoed off the cedar-paneled walls and danced around the huge stone pillars. Jewels flashed in the ladies' headdresses. Brightly colored robes, fringed in gold and cinched up with long, striped sashes, swished across the marble floor. Earrings dangled. Ankle chains jingled. Ezra could see it all from his hiding place under the table that bore the silver wine cups.

Suddenly a sharp pain shot through his hand and up his arm. "Ow!" he hissed. "Shub! You're on my little finger!"

"Sorry," said She'ar-Yashub, shifting his weight. Shub, as his friends called him, was tall for his age—nearly a span taller than Ezra, even though Ezra was more than two months older. It was a trait Shub had inherited from his father, the prophet Isaiah, but it didn't suit him as well as his famous parent—at least Ezra didn't think so. Isaiah was an imposing, daunting figure. Shub, on the other hand, was just gangly and clumsy—surprisingly so for an intelligent boy who played the harp and amused himself by writing poetry.

As Shub leaned to one side to remove his knee from Ezra's finger, his head jerked upward and bumped the underside of the table. *Bang!* The table shook. There was a light chime of ringing silver cups overhead.

"That was smart!" whispered Hezekiah, a stocky, ruddy-faced boy of 10; a boy who, in Ezra's opinion, spent too much time thinking and took everything way too seriously. Hezekiah could definitely be a pain. Still, he *was* the crown prince of Judah, and he *did* look up to the two older boys—especially Ezra. So he was worth keeping around.

"I was afraid of this," Hezekiah went on, glancing nervously at Ezra. "Now they'll catch us for sure!" He darted a deadly look at Shub.

Shub shrugged apologetically. "Sorry," he whispered. "I'm a musician—not a thief or a spy."

Afraid, thought Ezra. *Hezekiah is always afraid!* Well, maybe he had a good reason to be afraid. After all, if they *were* caught, their little game—secretly "crashing" a state dinner party and stuffing themselves with as much stolen food as possible—

probably wouldn't go over very well with King Ahaz. And Ezra would be in no end of trouble if his father, Tola, ever found out. Tola was Isaiah's right-hand man—an aristocratic statesman and staunch believer in the Lord who had helped the prophet found the Remnant, a righteous community of "true disciples" of Yahweh. It was a lot for a kid like Ezra to live down.

While these thoughts were passing through Ezra's head, the ringing of the cups died away. The sandaled feet of the adults who stood clustered near the table shuffled this way and that over the polished marble floor. A conversation just beyond the fringe of the tablecloth began to gather steam. Apparently no one had noticed the bump. Ezra heard Hezekiah breathe a sigh of relief.

"No, absolutely not!" said a gravel-throated man who was standing not more than two cubits away from their hiding place. "I wouldn't hesitate to say it to his face."

"The prophet Isaiah himself?" The second speaker sounded much older. "I take it you've never met him. Why, he literally thunders when he speaks of the penalty Judah will pay for the sin of chasing after other gods."

"Ha!" laughed the first man. "And what have all his thunderings come to? Things have never been better, I tell you. Turned my biggest profit ever in the copper trade this year. Ahaz knew what he was doing when he refurbished the high places and introduced the Syrian and Assyrian gods into the city."

"Don't count on it," said the older man. "Just look at Israel's history. Decisions like this have always led to . . . *unpleasant* consequences."

That's when Ezra saw his chance.

"Come on," he whispered, pointing to a long side table that stood over against the cedar-paneled west wall. "The really *good* stuff is over there."

Then, with a swift, sudden motion, he pulled the cloth aside and dashed into the open. The two other boys scuttled after him, crossing the marble floor on hands and knees. Ezra fixed his eyes firmly on their tantalizing goal: a sideboard loaded with all kinds of tasty appetizers. There were bowls of moist dates, platters of raisin cakes, pomegranates, small loaves of sweet bread, pressed figs, olives, and juicy little squares of hot, roasted lamb. He could almost taste it. Past the wine vat . . . just a little farther and . . .

Bang! Scrape! Inwardly, Ezra groaned. *Not again!* he thought.

But it was true. When he turned and looked over his shoulder, there sat poor Shub, the latch of his sandal caught on one of the claw-shaped feet of the huge silver wine vat. As he struggled to free himself, the vast container shuddered slightly, spilling a few drops of deep red liquid at the feet of a stout, important-looking man who was dipping out a measure of wine into a fashionable lady's silver cup.

"Wait! Let me do it," whispered Ezra. He grabbed his friend's foot and began fumbling with the leather sandal latch, all the while keeping a nervous eye on the stout man and fashionable lady, who fortunately seemed absorbed in their conversation. That was when it hit him.

Mother! Why hadn't he recognized her before? Her hair, perhaps . . . piled high on top of her head and wrapped with ribbons and chains of tiny gold rings. Ezra knew that his mother frequented affairs of this sort, but he really hadn't expected to see her at this one. Father hadn't said a word about it. He wondered if Father even knew. To make matters worse, the man filling his mother's cup was none other than King Ahaz himself! Ezra ducked, hoping to avoid being seen.

"It's regrettable, Jehudith," the king was saying in his golden voice, "that the gods should have given a charming woman like you such an obtuse husband."

Jehudith bent her head slightly and batted her long-lashed eyes. Her dangling silver earrings sparkled in the lamplight.

" 'Obtuse'—a very apt choice of words, Your Majesty," said another man, stepping up to join the conversation. He was a darkly handsome man with a trim black beard, wearing a kaftan of white linen and a scarlet turban. Ezra saw him lay a hand on his mother's arm and smile pleasantly into her face. "I might have used the term 'dense' myself."

Dense? My father? thought Ezra as he tugged and tugged at the leather thong. He didn't particularly like the sound of that, but there was no time to think about it now.

"Oh, Tola is a very intelligent man, Hanun," Ahaz went on. "Like his friend the prophet. But they are also both exceedingly stubborn. I say we can learn much from the Assyrians. Their gods have obviously been a great help to them. Surely they can help us, too."

One last pull, and the sandal latch came loose. "Got it!" whispered Ezra.

"My thoughts exactly, Your Majesty," said Hanun. "Why limit ourselves to *one* god? That's so—so *narrow.* Don't you agree, my dear Jehudith?"

"All right, Shub—*now!*" hissed Ezra.

"An astute observation, Hanun," he heard the king say as he and Shub crept away. "Why, I'm even of the opinion that the Assyrian gods may be the key to ridding us of the Assyrians themselves *and* their bothersome tribute. The fire of Molech's altar is especially powerful—as *I* have good reason to know . . ."

As the king's voice droned on, the boys reached the side table, seized a handful of dates apiece, and plunged to safety beneath the embroidered blue tablecloth. There they sat, feasting on stolen fruit and talking in hushed voices.

"Whew!" said Ezra, munching a date and readjusting the leather headband he always kept bound around his black curls. "That was a close one."

"I *told* you," Shub said. "This kind of thing is a little out of my field. I'm much better off at home with my *kinnor*." He smiled and took a bite out of a particularly plump date.

That's when Ezra caught sight of Hezekiah's face. He thought the king's son was looking strangely pale. "What's wrong with *you?*" he asked.

Hezekiah shut his eyes. "I couldn't help hearing what my father just said. About . . . *Molech*."

"What about it?"

Hezekiah just shivered and shook his head. "And that other man back there. Did you hear what *he* said? About the prophet and . . . *unpleasant consequences?*"

"Consequences?" laughed Ezra.

"Yes, Ezra," said Hezekiah, his cheeks red and a very serious look on his face. He paused, and it was as if a fog were lifting from his eyes. "I'm afraid we're going to get in big trouble for doing this. In spite of what you say. Don't you think so, Shub?"

Shub chewed thoughtfully. "It's possible. There are several ways of looking at it. On the one hand, as my father always says . . ."

"Your father!" snorted Ezra. "He's a fanatic, that's all. *She'ar-Yashub*—'A Remnant Shall Return.' Come on! Who would name a kid something like that?"

"*Your* dad would," answered Shub with an ironic smile. "*Ezra-Elohenu*—'A Help Is Our God.' "

"Don't remind me."

"But what if they're right?" Hezekiah managed to break into the conversation. "I mean, about God's law and consequences and all that. Maybe there really *is* a price to be paid for . . . for worshiping idols and . . . well, swiping food and stuff."

Ezra swallowed hard and scowled. "Do you *really* think that?"

"Don't you?"

"I'll tell you what *I* think. *I* think a kid can get away with *anything* if he's smart enough!" Then, smiling as if under a sudden inspiration, he added, "Watch this."

"Wait!" said Hezekiah. "Where are you going?"

But Ezra had already slipped out from under the table. Reaching up, he seized a pair of big, red pomegranates from a white ceramic bowl and headed back toward the wine vat. Dropping to his knees in front of the huge silver vessel, he cracked the hard, red rinds of the fruit against the floor, pried the pomegranates open, and crushed the tiny juice-filled beads inside against the marble tiles.

It was done in a moment. The next instant he was back in his hiding place, gulping down a mouthful of honey-raisin cake.

"What was that all about?" asked Hezekiah.

Ezra glanced at him out of the corner of his eye. "Just watch," he said with a grin.

They did. It wasn't long before Ahaz's chief cupbearer approached to replenish the guests' supply of drink. He was a stiff, dignified-looking man. His white tunic was smart and crisp. His gray head was held high. He carried a golden tray of silver cups on his uplifted palm. Ezra saw him smile at Ahaz, Jehudith, and Hanun as he passed their small discussion group.

In the next moment the cupbearer's smile gave way to a look of horror. That was when his left foot landed in the middle of the mass of crushed pomegranate and shot out from under him with all the swiftness of lightning. It was followed just as suddenly by his right foot. Ezra choked down a laugh as the man's entire body flew forward feet first. Cups flew in one direction, the tray in another. The tray bounced off Hanun's richly turbaned head and landed with a *bang* as it went skidding across the floor. There was a terrific splash, and before anyone knew what had happened, the dignified cupbearer was sitting in the wine vat, dripping with red liquid. Wine and pomegranate juice flowed across the white marble floor, staining the hems of the guests' robes a deep shade of reddish purple.

Everyone stared. For a brief moment silence reigned. Ezra fought to hold back his laughter. And then, from across the room—from out of the dripping wine vat—the angry, roving eyes of the cupbearer suddenly found a gap in the blue tablecloth and fixed themselves upon Ezra where he crouched hidden, his mouth full of roasted lamb.

"I told you so," moaned Hezekiah. "He sees us. Now we're caught for sure!"

"Just wait," whispered Ezra with a confident

smile. "It's not over yet. I can talk my way out of *anything!*"

"Your Majesty!" shouted the cupbearer. "Look! Under the table against the wall. It's your son and that hooligan of a troublemaker, Tola's boy!"

Instantly the entire party was in an uproar. Guards in brassy cuirasses and pointed helmets descended upon the sideboard and dragged the boys from their shadowy hiding place. Everything became a blur as Ezra was pulled to his feet and shoved in the direction of the king. When he came to a stop, he found himself standing in front of the king and Jehudith. Beside him were Hezekiah and Shub.

"Better make it good!" whispered Hezekiah through clenched teeth.

"Well, well!" said the king as a hush descended over the great hall. "What have we here?" He paused to hiccup, then bent down and stared sternly into the boys' faces one by one. "Hezekiah?" he went on, glaring angrily at his son. "What is the meaning of this? What were you boys doing under that table? And who made this mess all over the floor? Hmmm?"

"Father, I—I—" stammered the prince.

"Hezekiah, if you think for one minute that I—"

Quickly Ezra sized up the situation. This was

a tight spot for sure. His status as a hero was hanging in the balance. His theory was about to be disproved. Worst of all, his friend was about to be blamed for something *he* had done. Well, he'd told Hezekiah that he could talk his way out of anything, and if ever there were a time to start talking, it was now. So he blurted out the first thing that came into his head.

"Please don't, Your Majesty," he said, interrupting the king's swelling tirade. "It's not his fault."

Ahaz frowned. "Not his fault? Well, then whose fault *is* it?"

"Mine."

Ezra saw his mother turn pale. It was a bold stroke, but he had his reasons for believing that it just might work. Hezekiah turned and stared at him in disbelief. Shub looked at his feet and scratched his nose.

"*Your* fault?" said Ahaz, eyeing the boy narrowly. He hiccuped again. "Hmmm. Tola's boy, isn't it?"

"Yes, Your Majesty."

"Son of our sweet Jehudith, here?"

"The same, Your Majesty."

A murmur arose and wafted around the hall. Ezra sensed that every eye in the place was fixed upon him. He trembled inside, wondering if he had miscalculated. And then, slowly—ever so slowly—a lopsided smile broke across Ahaz's face.

"Well," said the king with a chuckle, "I see no reason to make any more of this affair than it warrants. Boys will be boys, eh? And now I think *you* boys had better leave us . . . before something worse happens, hmm?" He hiccuped again and waved them off.

"Yes, Your Majesty," said Ezra. Then, grabbing his two friends by their sleeves, he hurried from the hall as fast as he could go.

"Like the way I handled that?" said Ezra triumphantly when they were standing together at the palace gate. "I told you guys!"

Shub scratched his ear. "I'm still not sure how you did that," he said.

"Easy. The king's had too much to drink, and an honest confession was the last thing he was expecting. It's the old element of surprise. I *knew* it would work."

Hezekiah looked up at his friend with a confused frown. "I guess I owe you one, Ezra. But I still can't help thinking that your tricks are going to catch up with you one of these days."

"Even after what just happened? *Aauughh!* What does it take to convince some people?"

Shub looked amused.

"I'm sorry," said the prince, staring down at his sandals. "I keep thinking about the prophet and . . . what that man said."

Ezra heaved a frustrated sigh. "Looks like it's time I got serious with you, Hezekiah."

"Serious?"

"That's right. Time we started your education in earnest."

"Education?"

"Mm-hm." Ezra relaxed, smiled, leaned his shoulder against the wall, and straightened his headband. "You just wait. By the time we get through, you'll see that all this grown-up talk about gods and rules and judgment and consequences is just a big joke. You'll *know* I'm right. If he's smart enough and lucky enough, a kid can get away with *anything*. You'll see!"

CHAPTER 2

It wasn't far from the palace to the house of Tola ben Abihu. Even so, it took Ezra nearly an hour to get home that evening. He had a long, aimless walk through the gathering darkness. After all, there was no reason to hurry. He wasn't exactly sure what to expect when he got to his father's door, but he was pretty certain it wouldn't be pleasant. Mother was at the king's dinner, he knew that. That meant that Father would be in a mood. And *that* meant that Ezra would probably have to listen to a lecture about idolatry and the warnings of the prophet Isaiah. No wonder he felt like dawdling.

The sun had gone down in the softly glowing distance beyond Jerusalem's western wall, and the first stars were just winking out of the deepening blue overhead. Clay oil lamps were being lit and set into niches in the walls of the houses that lined the winding cobbled lanes. He could see their tiny flames blinking through the latticework shutters over the windows as he passed.

Ezra sighed, straightened his leather headband, and kicked a big rock that lay in his path. He *had* wanted to look for some fun in the streets with the others before going home, but Hezekiah had turned him down. Said he wasn't in the mood. *That Hezekiah!* thought Ezra. As for Shub, he had told Ezra that his parents and younger brother were holding another meeting of the Remnant somewhere in the neighborhood that night, and that he wanted to go home and practice his harp while he had the house to himself. "They don't always appreciate my music," he had explained.

So Ezra was left alone. He kicked the rock again and shuffled on. When at last he could see the flickering lamplight in the window of his own house, he brought his feet to a stop, folded his arms, and leaned up against the wall of a house. As he eased his back against the stones, bits of loose mortar crumbled and fell to the ground making a skittering sound on the pavement. *Consequences*, he thought. *Your tricks will catch up with you someday.* He laughed to himself. *What's the big deal? What does it matter, anyway? Can't a kid have a little fun without everybody jumping down his throat?* He stooped down, picked up a rock, and, with an angry grimace, heaved it into the darkness.

"Ai! Ow!" came the voice of an elderly woman through the gloom. Ezra froze at the sound. The blood rushed into his face. He hadn't meant to *hit* anyone with the rock; he hadn't even realized that anyone was *there*.

The voice cried out again: "Who did that? Come out, you young ruffians!" Ezra took to his heels, darted down a narrow side alley, and came around to the door of his house by a roundabout back way.

He wasn't expecting what he found there. The doorway was jammed with people. Ezra knew at once what it was: The meeting of the Remnant that Shub had mentioned was taking place at *his* house! And it was just adjourning. His father, Tola, a short, bulky man, stood in front of the house at the edge of the street, taking leave of his guests.

Ezra knew them all by sight. There, for instance, was Shub's goody-goody younger brother, Maher-Shalal-Hash-Baz, talking with Tola for all the world as if he were some kind of miniature adult. Maher-Shalal-Hash-Baz—"Swift-Spoil-Speedy-Prey." And *some* people thought *Ezra-*

Elohenu was a strange name. At nine years old, Maher was already almost as big a pain in the neck as his father—a junior prophet in the making. *He* made Hezekiah look like a wild and crazy troublemaker. Always talking about "the Lord" this and "the Lord" that and "the Son of David." It was enough to make a kid want to run off and join the Assyrian army.

Then there was Shub and Maher's mother, Abigail—a petite, energetic, frizzy-haired woman who stood in the doorway just behind her boy. Most men called their wives things like *shoshanna* (lily-flower) or *yonah* (dove) or *yephath-mareh* (fair one), but Isaiah referred to *her* as *nebiah*— "the prophetess." It was all just a little too weird for Ezra.

He watched them emerge from the house one by one and wondered what he ought to do. After weighing his options he decided that the best thing would be to try to slip inside as the members of the Remnant crowded *out*. That way, his father would be too busy saying good-bye to notice him. Having made his resolve, Ezra closed in on the house.

Closer and closer he edged. He could see Tola listening intently to an elderly woman who was weeping and gesturing angrily and talking rapidly about something. *Now or never!* he thought; and with that he made a sudden attempt to duck behind the woman and push his way inside. But just as he thought he was home free, he found himself looking up into the face of a tall, imposing figure: the prophet Isaiah himself.

"Well. Hello, Ezra," said the prophet. His long, dark beard, streaked with strands of silver-gray, swept down over his chest as he bent to smile at the boy. "We missed you tonight!"

Ezra gulped. He tried to look cool and collected as he gazed up into the man's deep-set eyes. But his heart was pounding as if it would jump up out of his throat at any moment. "Ah . . . yes. Hello . . . *adoni* Isaiah . . . sir . . ."

Just then he felt the grip of a thick hand on his left shoulder. He turned to see his father's nose an inch away from his own.

"Ezra," said Tola in a frighteningly low and controlled tone, "let's go inside for a little chat."

Ezra was caught without a comeback.

Tola clamped his other hand down on his son's right shoulder and turned to the prophet. "I'm sorry, Isaiah. We'll speak again tomorrow."

"Certainly, Tola. Good night," said the prophet. Gradually, the smile on his face gave way to a sober expression made up of gathering wrinkles and creases. "Come, Abigail, Maher." Isaiah took his shawl-clad wife by the arm. Then, followed by their son, they turned and disappeared into the night.

Meanwhile, Tola had not released his grip on Ezra. As soon as the prophet and his family were gone, he gently guided the boy into the house and shut the door.

"Sit," he said, still in the same carefully controlled tone. He pointed to a leather-covered stool that stood in the corner of the small, stone-floored entry hall that led to the main part of the house.

Now what? thought Ezra. Assuming a nonchalant, unhurried air, he sauntered over to the stool and sat down.

"Ezra, have you been throwing rocks again?" asked his father.

"Rocks?"

"Old Hephzibah was just hit on the arm by a rock. A big one. Near our house. I can't tell for sure, but she acts as if she's badly hurt."

Ezra was beginning to tremble. "Father! You think *I* would do a thing like that?"

"What I *think* isn't the question. Did you do it?"

"I didn't do anything!" said Ezra, assuming an angry, offended air. "I didn't throw any rock at anybody." This was true in Ezra's mind, since he hadn't meant to throw the rock *at* anyone.

Tola cocked an eyebrow and looked at his son. "I see. Well, then, why don't we move on to another subject. Perhaps you wouldn't mind telling me what happened at the king's dinner party tonight?"

Ezra felt the blood rush to his heart. *How can he know about that?* "What dinner party?"

"You know very well what dinner party," replied Tola.

Ezra could see his father's round cheeks coloring above his gray-streaked beard. He could hear the hint of a tremor in his voice. How it had happened he didn't know, but he'd been caught. The realization turned him sullen and resentful.

"What do *you* know about any old dinner party?" he said casting his eyes down at the floor and readjusting his headband.

"Enough. Elisabeth, one of the king's maid-servants, joined the meeting of the Remnant when her evening chores were completed." Tola bent down and gave his son a piercing stare. "She took me aside and told me everything."

"So? What do you care?"

That was when his father's anger suddenly burst its carefully set boundaries. His voice rose and swelled. "What do I *care?*" he shouted. "Am I not to care about my own son's actions? Actions that bring shame upon his father's household?"

"That's all that matters to you, isn't it, Father," said Ezra without looking up. "*Your* shame. *Your* reputation. Like I'm just some kind of an extension of *you*. Well, I'm not! I'm myself!"

"Have you no respect, Ezra?" Tola went on, as if he hadn't heard the boy. "If not for the king, then for the prophet and the Remnant and everything it represents? Elisabeth said you made a shambles of the party with your antics. How can you do this to me? What a way for Tola's son to behave." He bowed his head and passed a hand over his eyes. "As if your mother's unfaithfulness to the Lord weren't enough," he added quietly.

"Leave Mother out of it," said Ezra bitterly, looking up into his father's face at last. "She can do what she likes. Why do you think that everybody has to be just like you? Even the name you gave me is about *your* beliefs, not mine."

"Ezra," said Tola, his voice dropping again, "it is not a question of *my* beliefs or *your* beliefs. It is a question of hearing and obeying the Holy One of Israel. It is a question of *truth*. Of knowing the True and Living God! 'Hear, O Israel: The Lord our God, the Lord is one!' There will be terrible consequences for those who forsake the Lord and follow false gods. Haven't you heard what happened to Aaron's sons Nadab and Abihu when they offered up strange fire in the desert of Sinai? The prophet said it again as he was teaching tonight—'this will you have of My hand, says the Lord. You will lie down in anguish!' "

Ezra jumped to his feet. "Then what about King Ahaz? *He* believes in the other gods. Don't *you* have any respect for *him?*"

"Of course I respect him—as my king. But he is wrong, Ezra. Sadly and tragically wrong. He will pay a heavy price for his sins one day." He shook his head and added, "Perhaps he already has."

"Yeah, right. Isaiah has been saying that for as long as I can remember. And nothing bad has *ever* happened to King Ahaz."

"Believe me, my son," said Tola sadly. "The day will come. The Lord's timing is not as our own; nor is He a man, that He should delay to strike the wicked in . . ."

But Ezra didn't want to hear any more. "I've had enough of 'consequences' and 'judgments' and all that stuff about the Remnant! And nothing bad is going to happen to Mother just because she went to the king's dinner party. Why can't you just lighten up a little bit?" With that, he turned and stormed out of the entry hall.

"Ezra!" shouted his father as he went. "You're not to leave this house for a week!"

But Ezra wasn't listening. He could almost feel the skin of his face steaming with frustration and anger as he ran through the house. He ducked under the low arch that led to his room, pushed through the dark-blue curtain that hung over the doorway, and flung himself down on the reed sleeping mat in the corner. He didn't bother to light a lamp, but lay there staring up into the darkness, breathing heavily, his hands behind his head. The events of the evening ran through his head scene by scene: Hezekiah's sober, serious face under the table; his mother and the king and Hanun, their heads bent together in conversation about the Assyrian gods; the pomegranates and the spilled wine and the eyes of the crowd; King Ahaz's indulgent smile; a rock flying through the darkness; the prophet's bearded face; his father's weighty words.

Suddenly Ezra laughed. "Consequences," he said to himself out loud, getting up and going over to the little window. There he stood, staring out at the darkened city through one of the spaces in the lattice. *I'll show them. I'll show them all! Nothing* bad is going to happen to Mother or me or the king or anybody else. I meant what I said to Hezekiah, and I'm going to prove it. They haven't seen anything yet.

CHAPTER 3

W hy, Jehudith?" said Tola. "*Why* must you go out again?"

It was the following evening, and Ezra was listening to his parents go through the same old tired argument. The timing couldn't have been worse—he'd made secret arrangements to meet Shub and Hezekiah after dark, and the evening was wearing away.

"This is your home," Ezra's father went on, twisting the edge of his brown robe between his hands. "Your family is here—your son, the husband who loves you. *Why* are you never content to remain at home with us?"

Tola stood in the small entry hall at the front of the house, pleading with his wife, a look of desperation on his face. Jehudith was wrapped and veiled in a cloak of midnight blue bordered with a stripe of Tyrian purple. In her right hand she held a small pitcher-shaped clay lamp. Her left hand rested on the door latch. Gold bracelets hung with silver baubles jingled at her wrists. Matching earrings dangled at each side of her face—a surprisingly young and pretty face for a woman of middle age.

Ezra hung back in the shadows, beyond the circle of the lamplight. He hated it when his parents fought like this. The edge in Tola's voice cut him like the edge of a knife. He didn't like to hear his father speak to his mother in that tone. After all, Mother had a right do as she pleased—that's what Ezra always said. But then he had to admit that he, too, hated it when she went out, as she did almost every other night. Somehow, it always gave him a hollow, sick feeling in the pit of his stomach to see her leave. And yet he knew that there could never be a moment's peace in the house as long as she was there.

"I really don't see why it concerns you, Tola," said Jehudith in a cold and distant voice. Ezra could see the light of the lamp gleaming on her white teeth and glinting off her shiny red lips from within the folds of her veil. "I should think you'd be too busy with the Remnant to notice or care whether I stay or go. And I *will* go, for I want to experience new things. I want to taste the gifts of the gods. Ahaz is a brilliant, forward-thinking

king. He's done wonders for Judah. I for one wish to follow his lead. And I won't let you hold me back!"

Without another word, she lifted the latch, opened the door, and slipped out into the night. Tola covered his grizzled head with his hands and stalked off into the interior of the house, muttering to himself.

It was the opportunity Ezra had been waiting for. As soon as he could no longer hear the sounds of his father's frustrated fumings, he covered himself in a cloak of his own—dark gray so as to make himself as "invisible" as possible—and slipped through the door. In the next moment he was out in the gray-cobbled, high-walled canyon of the street, darting from shadow to shadow, his sandals slapping the stones.

He found Shub, just as they'd arranged, at the dark, arched corner at the end of Mishneh Street. He, too, was dressed in a dark cloak. One of his father's, to judge by the way it trailed along the ground. His head was bare except for its natural covering of wild black hair. Cradled in the crook of his right arm he carried his precious *kinnor*, a small harp. It was a simple instrument: a rectangular sounding box of cypress wood, two upward-curving arms of ash, a cross-beam of the same wood, and 10 strings of dried gut. Apparently Shub was looking forward to a night of music and dancing.

"Hey!" said Shub as Ezra emerged from the shadows. "Where's your tambourine?"

"You know I don't have a tambourine," said Ezra impatiently. "Where's Hezekiah?"

"He'll be here," said Shub softly. As he spoke, he caressed the strings of the *kinnor* the way Ezra had sometimes seen his father caress his mother's hair—back when they were on better terms.

Hezekiah arrived shortly, draped in a very ragged and dirty piece of sackcloth. In compliance with Ezra's instructions, he had smeared his ruddy face with a handful of ashes so that he looked every inch the wild and homeless street urchin. Shub laughed when he saw him, but Ezra eyed Hezekiah up and down and nodded a solemn approval.

"Good," he said. "It wouldn't do for anyone to recognize you where we're going tonight."

"Where *are* we going, anyway?" asked the prince, looking up at the older boy with a frown and a wrinkled forehead.

"To a place I've always wanted to see at night," answered Ezra with a confident smile. "The *bamah*—the high place—in Ophel."

"Ophel? The high place?" said Shub. "You mean the pagan altar?"

"That's right. I told you there'd be music, didn't I? There's supposed to be a festival there tonight. It'll be fun!"

Without another word he set off, leading the others southward along the winding lane that led to *Ha'iyr-David*, David's City, the most ancient part of Jerusalem, and beyond it to the Potsherd Gate and the Hinnom Valley. Above them loomed the dark and lofty grandeur of the temple, and beyond that the high roofs of the royal palace. They moved as silently as cats, keeping to the shadows.

Ezra was in high spirits, pleased as he could be with his own resourcefulness. He'd show them. He'd teach Hezekiah once and for all that a kid didn't need anything but his own brains. They'd visit the high place. They'd eat and dance and sing and have a great time. And nothing bad would happen to them. Then he'd be a bigger hero than ever. It was a good feeling.

For some reason the face of Shub's younger brother popped into his mind as he made his way down the street in the moonlight, thinking these pleasant thoughts. That pudgy, snotty face, topped with a bush of ridiculous black fuzz. He was glad that he was so much wiser and cleverer than that insufferable bore of a mommy's boy. *Maher-Shalal-Hash-Baz*, he thought scornfully. *Give me a break*. He turned to Shub, who was walking at his side, and said it aloud in a scornful tone. "Maher-Shalal-Hash-Baz. Swift-Spoil-Speedy-Prey! What's that supposed to mean, anyway?"

"It means," Shub answered carefully, "that if the people don't shape up, the Assyrian army will swoop down and make fish bait out of them. Just another way of saying that your sins catch up with you. My father's very fond of that kind of thing."

Tell me about it! thought Ezra, choosing to ignore the comment.

The moon went behind a blanket of cloud as they trudged forward. From that point on the night seemed to grow darker with every step they took. They didn't dare carry a lamp for fear of attracting attention. Every so often they stopped and peered ahead as darker blobs of blackness loomed up or lunged out at them from the heart of shallower pools of murk. They would laugh at themselves nervously when they realized that the blob was nothing but a cat or the swaying limb of a stunted acacia tree. But Ezra couldn't help wishing that the moon would come out again. He'd never realized that Jerusalem could be so dark at night. He didn't *really* know the night side of the city at all.

On they walked, staying close to the wall. As they came around a bend in the lane, Ezra could see an orange glow rising beyond the dark shapes of the huddled houses and shops. The glow pulsed, undulated, and reflected dully along the rough vertical edge of a tall structure of stone. The Tower of Ophel.

"That's it!" said Ezra excitedly. "See? There's a fire on the altar! The high place is just below the tower. There's an alley that turns to the left just before you get to David's City. It'll take us straight there. Not much farther now. Follow me!"

Quickening his pace, Ezra pushed on. But he was stopped in his tracks by a thud, a shout, and the jangling of harp strings at his back.

"*Ummpphh!* My *kinnor!*"

Oh, no, thought Ezra. *He tripped again!* Wheeling around and peering through the darkness, he searched for Shub and found him lying on his back, the precious harp clutched tightly to his chest. His long legs were sprawled across another dark shape that lay beneath him on the ground. At first Ezra thought that Shub had fallen over

Hezekiah. But no—Hezekiah was standing right beside him.

"What happened, Ezra?" asked the prince, staring down at the two prostrate figures.

"Oh, it's just that clumsy Shub again," he answered. "What did you trip over this time, Shub?"

He bent down to get a closer look at the unlucky individual who lay squirming beneath Shub's long legs. It was hard to see anything now that the light of the moon had gone. Closer he leaned, and closer. Then, with a gasp, he recognized the face at last.

It was Old Hephzibah!

CHAPTER 4

Help me," moaned Old Hephzibah in a pitiful voice, stretching out her hand to Ezra. "Help an old woman who has lost the use of her arm!"

Ezra stood and gaped. He pulled the hood of his cloak closer around his face. Old Hephzibah! Dressed in black, and with her arm in a sling. The very *last* person he'd expected to see that night. He felt he ought to speak to her, but he didn't know what to say. He knew he should help her, but he was afraid of being recognized. Instead of doing either, he reached down, took Shub by the hand, and pulled him to his feet.

"Come on!" he whispered fiercely. "Let's get out of here!"

Just then he felt a pair of strong hands seize him by the shoulder. They gripped him like a vise, so sharply that a bolt of fiery pain shot down his arm like a flash of lightning. Then they spun him around. Suddenly he found himself staring into a face that looked for all the world like a skull wrapped in a discolored sheepskin. The mouth opened and a foul odor of red wine mixed with stale cheese invaded Ezra's nostrils.

"You heard her, boy," said a gruff voice. "The old lady needs help. How about it? A scrap of bread for her and a few coins for *me!* Eh?"

Suddenly the moon jumped out from behind the clouds again. In her silvery light Ezra saw the flash of a dull blade before his face.

"Let me go!" he shouted, struggling to free himself from the man's grasp.

"Thief! Thief!" shouted Hezekiah. In the next instant he and Shub were at Ezra's side fighting furiously to rescue their friend. Ezra heard the man cry out as Hezekiah landed a solid punch on his bony jaw. The strings of the harp sounded in sympathy as Shub, too, got in a swift kick. It was too much for Ezra's assailant. Howling in pain, he released his grip on the boy and fled into the darkness, cursing as he went.

"Whoa!" muttered Shub, breathing heavily and checking his precious *kinnor* for damage. "You didn't tell us it would be like *this!* I thought we were going to have *fun* tonight."

"Don't worry," said Ezra shakily, dusting himself off, straightening his leather headband, and pulling his hood back up over his head. "We *will*."

Old Hephzibah twisted and turned, groveling upon the ground. "*Unnhhh!*" she groaned.

"Ezra," said Hezekiah, taking his friend by the arm, "what about *her*? Don't you think we should . . . ?"

"Yeah," put in Shub. "My father always says that poor widows deserve . . ."

"Not now, *hamor*," hissed Ezra, a little more vehemently than was necessary. "We're almost there!"

"Don't call me a donkey," said Shub.

"Well, then, don't preach a sermon. We've got to keep going or it'll be too late!" And without allowing his friends to say another word, he pulled them away from the old woman and once more in the direction of the orange glow, trembling inside more violently than he would have liked to admit.

They reached the dirty side alley Ezra had mentioned and turned into it. Here the blackness of the night was broken at intervals by the glow of lamps, glimpsed dimly through broken window lattices and torn curtains. There were torches, too, and fires burning in clay pots and bronze braziers under the cover of tattered awnings and low, arched doorways.

"Don't be scared," Ezra whispered nervously to Hezekiah, who walked hunched over at his side. "It's just one of those poor neighborhoods you're always hearing about. That's all." But inside his only thought was to get out of that alley as quickly as he could.

Around the fires huddled the dark shapes of strange, gaunt men and women, their faces hideous and unnatural in the blood-red light of the flames. A yellow-skinned, black-haired woman, her head bound with strands of gold coins, her face aglow with stripes of red paint, turned and beckoned to them with a crooked finger as they passed. Ezra pretended not to see her. A sallow-faced man with a pale, stringy beard studied them closely out of his single eye. Little boys shouted and assaulted them with handfuls of rotten dates. Soon they put all thought of dignity aside and began to run.

As the end of the alley came in sight, Ezra became aware of an odd fluttering sensation in the pit of his stomach. Not that he was afraid. There was nothing to be afraid of, he told himself. *He* was clever enough to get himself and his friends through *anything*. Even this.

They reached their goal under a juicy hail of some other kind of fruit—probably pomegranates, Ezra guessed—and emerged into a large, open square. Directly ahead of them, leaning menacingly over the scene in the lurid light, was the Tower of Ophel itself, a fortification of massive stone built for the city's defense by Hezekiah's grandfather, Jotham. At its base, in the exact center of the plaza—a space contained on one side by the city wall and on the three remaining sides by the surrounding shops and houses—was a sight that took their breath away.

"*Hoi!*" exclaimed the prince, leaning on Ezra's arm. "This *does* look fun!"

It did. The place was filled with people dressed in bright, multicolored clothing. Some of the women wore loosely wrapped, gauzy pastel robes such as Ezra had sometimes seen on foreigners from Ammon and Philistia. Headbands of shimmering gold dangled from their foreheads and down over their noses. Their feet and arms were bare, and many of them had painted the skin of their faces and legs. Men dressed in the Assyrian or Egyptian style, bare-chested and in wraparound loincloths of embroidered wool, dashed here and there with torches and platters of food, some of them wearing masks of hideous or hilarious design. From what Ezra could see, the crowd was made up of people from every class in

Jerusalem: wealthy officials and courtiers; well-to-do merchants; honest working folk; dirty, sunken-cheeked beggars. All of them were laughing and talking merrily.

Some of the people had spread blankets on the ground and were reclining in groups of threes or fours, dining eagerly on bunches of grapes and raisin cakes. Others were downing great silver cups of wine. Still others were dancing to the beat of the *tabor* and the music of the pipes and flutes. The air was filled with smoke and cooking smells and the confused jangle of hundreds of talking and shouting voices.

Ranged around the square were ranks of wooden poles, 10 to 15 feet in height, each one carved from top to bottom with strange, intertwining shapes. Some of the poles had ribbons of white, purple, or scarlet cloth fluttering from their tips. It was like a forest of bright color and endless motion. *Asherah poles*, Ezra said to himself when he saw them. *So that's what they look like.*

"This is what I've been waiting for!" said Shub, gripping his *kinnor* tightly under his arm and heading for the nearest group of musicians. "I'll see you two a little later."

"What's *that?*" asked Hezekiah, tightening his grip on Ezra's arm and pointing, wide-eyed, to a pyramid of stone steps that culminated in a peak of curiously carved stone and a tongue of bright flame. The fire leapt and bowed, casting an eerie glow over the entire scene, illuminating the tower and even painting the distant walls of the temple a dusky orange.

"That's what we came for," answered Ezra in an excited whisper. "The high place! The altar of Baal and Asherah. And see what I told you? All of these people are having a great time. Nothing bad is happening to any of them."

"It *does* look like fun," Hezekiah said hesitantly. "Do you think we could get some food?"

"Why not?" laughed Ezra. "Come on! What are we waiting for?"

With that they plunged into the thick of the festive crowd. Ezra's spirits were high, his heart light. The evening *had* gotten off to a rough start, he told himself, but it was all going to be worth it now. This was the payoff. He laughed out loud as a bare-chested man in a satiny red turban slapped him on the back and offered him a hunk of roasted meat, still on the bone, sizzling and dripping with red juices.

"Straight from the sacrifice," the man said, his narrow black eyes sparkling. "Share it around, share it around!"

Ezra and Hezekiah sat down on a thick, striped rug of red and white strands of wool, holding the shank of meat between them. Greedily they bent to it, tearing the succulent flesh from the bone, scattering spots of grease and blood down the fronts of their cloaks and over the carpet.

"Hey!" laughed Ezra. "Look at Shub!"

It was obvious that the prophet's son was in his glory. There he stood, in the middle of a group of prancing, capering celebrants, plucking at the strings of his *kinnor* in a fit of pure pleasure. Through the rhythmic flash of the dancers' bare arms and legs, Ezra and Hezekiah could see him, a look of ecstasy on his long, high-cheekboned face, his hair wilder and more uncontrolled than they had ever seen it before. *Yes*, thought Ezra, wiping his chin and licking his lips, *I'm really glad we came.*

That's when he saw a face—a face he had not expected to see in that wild place. Perhaps it was the surprise of seeing it there, combined with the unusual way in which the face was framed—in a headdress curiously like that of an Egyptian nobleman, with a bold stripe of red paint across the forehead and eyes—that kept him from recognizing it at first. But recognize it he did. When he did, so great was his shock that he dropped his end of the shank bone and grabbed Hezekiah by the shoulder.

"Hezekiah!" he said in a sharp whisper, pointing with his other hand. "Look! That man who was with your father at the dinner the other night—Hanun! Does *he* worship at the high place?"

"Why not?" said the prince with a shrug. "Just about everyone at Court does."

For a moment Ezra feared that Hanun would recognize them. But he soon came to realize that there was no danger of that. The noble courtier's attention was absorbed, his eyes fixed upon the bright eyes of a veiled woman whom he was leading by the arm, a woman dressed in a cloak of midnight blue edged with Tyrian purple. Reeling and swaying in time with the music, the two of them passed very close to the spot where Ezra and Hezekiah were sitting. That was when Ezra heard a voice—a melodic voice and a silvery laugh.

"No, you silly man," the voice said with a giggle. "I certainly won't—not unless you ask me *nicely!*"

Then the two figures slipped away together, through the forest of Asherah poles and into the heart of the heaving, dancing crowd.

With a strange, sinking feeling in the pit of his

stomach, Ezra released his grip on Hezekiah and dropped his hands to his sides.

"Hezekiah," he said flatly, "go get Shub. I think we'd better go home."

"Home?" said Hezekiah, looking up from the hunk of meat in surprise. "But why? We just got here."

"Don't be stupid!" said Ezra irritably, shaking himself and straightening his leather headband. "It's getting late. I don't want my father to find out that I've been here. Now go on!"

He got to his feet, wiping his greasy hands on his cloak as the bewildered Hezekiah scurried over to Shub. Ezra stared down at his fingers, sticky with blood and fat. He shook himself again and tried to believe that it must have been his imagination.

The woman's voice had sounded exactly like his mother's.

CHAPTER 5

Ezra awoke late the next morning to the sound of a raven complaining raucously in an almond tree just outside his window. "Get up! Get up!" the rude bird seemed to say.

Somewhere out in the street children were shouting and playing a game of "wedding-and-funeral"—he could tell by the sound of their piping on a little wooden flute. Beyond them, from some place even farther away, came the faint notes of a harp. *Shub's already up and at it*, he thought disgustedly.

He raised himself on one elbow and pushed the dark curls out of his eyes. Already the sun was high enough to dart sharp little javelins of light down through the spaces in the window lattice and straight into his face. Why did it have to be so bright? The light was offensive to him. It reflected off the ceiling and bounced off the walls. It revealed every crack, dip, and bump in the whitewashed mud plaster with which the inside of his room was covered. Ezra groaned and shoved his knuckles into his eye sockets. Then he lay down again and covered his head with the woolen blanket.

That's when he heard another sound—a sound smaller and softer than any of the others, and much closer. It was the curtain at his door swishing aside. This was followed by the pad of footsteps crossing the stone-flagged floor of the room. Then came a tug at the blanket.

"Ezra—are you going to sleep the day away?" His father's voice was gentle and quiet, but something about it made the boy jump inside. He threw off the blanket and sat straight up.

"I *am* up!" he said loudly. "I mean, I've *been* up for a while, only I just didn't want to *get* up—that's all."

The amused twinkle in Tola's eye was like a mirror in which Ezra was forced to look at the ridiculous image of his own confusion. There was the slightest hint of a smile playing at the corners of his father's mouth. That bothered Ezra. He hated it when his father shouted at him, but it was that ironic smile of his that made him *really* angry.

"Here," said Tola, reaching for Ezra's rough-spun yellow and ocher tunic where it lay on a stool next to the wall—just where Ezra had left it when he came in during the small hours of the morning. "Get dressed, and we'll have some breakfast."

Tola picked up the garment. Beneath it lay the gray woolen cloak Ezra had worn to the high place, the smeared grease and blood from the roasted calf shank clearly evident down its front side. Seeing it, his father stopped and stared for a brief moment with parted lips and raised eyebrows. Then he simply tossed the tunic to his son, saying, "Come on. The food's waiting in the other room."

Compared with Ezra's cramped sleeping quarters, the main room of the house was spacious and airy. There were two arched windows looking out into the street. The floor was of stone and the walls were of whitewashed plaster. Overhead, the roof was supported by six bare rafter poles of oak. In the center of the room Ezra's father had spread out a mat of woven reeds. On the mat lay a wooden bowl of goat's milk, a platter of disk-shaped barley loaves, and another bowl of *leben,* or soft white cheese.

"Sit. Eat," said Tola. He himself sat cross-legged on the mat and reached for the platter of bread. Ezra followed his example, watching his father warily.

Then, with a sudden jolt, Ezra remembered something. "Where's mother?" he asked.

"Still asleep," his father answered, calmly breaking a circular loaf down the middle. "She came in even later than you did," he added without looking up.

"*Me?*" said Ezra, dropping his own loaf in his lap. He'd taken every precaution to make sure that no one heard him come home. "What do you mean? Are you accusing me—?"

"Ezra," said Tola, looking straight at his son, "there's no need to shout. Your thirteenth birthday is not far away. Let's reason together like men."

"That'll be the day," scoffed Ezra. "To you I'm still a baby. To you I've got no life of my own . . . and neither does Mother!"

Ezra thought he saw his father wince. But all Tola said was, "I've been thinking about what you said the other night. I think I understand how you feel."

"What *I* said?"

"Yes. About being yourself instead of an extension of me. And about your name. I know how hard it must be for you to . . . to be *my* son."

Ezra took a bite of bread and chewed it slowly, staring up at his father's bearded face. He didn't know what to say. He wasn't sure what was coming.

"The prophet feels very strongly," Tola went on after a moment, "*I* feel very strongly, that we *must* raise up reminders for the coming generation . . . reminders that the Lord, *He* is God. Otherwise all is lost. We must *be* those reminders. Isaiah stated it so very clearly in one of the earliest speeches he ever gave in the temple courts. That was years and years ago, before you were born, but I remember it as if it were yesterday:

> *Bind up the testimony and seal up the law*
> *among my disciples.*
> *I will wait for the Lord, who is hiding his face*
> *from the house of Jacob.*
> *I will put my trust in him.*
>
> *Here am I, and the children the Lord has given me. We are signs and symbols in Israel from the Lord Almighty, who dwells on Mount Zion.*

"That, you see," his father concluded, "is why we've given you names like 'A Remnant Shall Return' and 'A Help Is Our God.' We want the people to remember, every time they see you, that

God is God and that He does not change from one generation to the next!"

"That's great for *you*, I guess," said Ezra bitterly. "But what about us? What about me and Shub? What if we don't want to be 'signs and symbols'?"

"Ezra, it is not a question of what we want. As the prophet Isaiah says—"

"What do I care what Isaiah says?" shouted Ezra. "He's just an old fanatic, that's all! Remember when he walked around the city barefoot and in a loincloth for three years? Is that what you call sane?"

Tola laid the rest of his loaf on the mat and stared at it thoughtfully. After a pause he continued in an even quieter voice.

"A 'fanatic,' you say. Yes. Perhaps you have good reason to think so. But do you know what it is like for a man," and at this he looked up and fixed his son with his calm, dark eyes, "to be owned by Another? To be no longer his own? Do you know what Isaiah saw in the temple while he was still a very young man?"

"How would I know?"

"It was the year King Uzziah died. Young Isaiah had gone in to pray before the altar. Suddenly the whole place was filled with wings and smoke and a living stream of blinding light, like the flowing skirts of a great fiery royal robe, pouring, cascading down from the throne of God. Everything started shaking and trembling! And seraphim were shouting, 'Holy! Holy! Holy!' "

Ezra stopped chewing and stared. "So what did he do?"

"He didn't know what to do," answered Tola. "He just said, 'Woe to me! For I am a man of unclean lips!' That's how it made him feel. And then he saw one of the seraphs take a hot coal from the altar with a pair of tongs. And the angel brought the coal over to Isaiah and reached out and touched his lips with it!"

"With a *hot* coal?"

"Yes! And the angel said, 'See, this has touched your lips; your guilt is taken away and your sin atoned for.' And then Isaiah heard the voice of the Lord Himself saying, 'Whom shall I send? And who will go for us?' So he said, 'Here am I. Send me!'

"So you see," Tola concluded slowly after another pause, "Isaiah has a good reason for being a 'fanatic,' as you call him. He's *seen* the Lord! He belongs to Him completely. And that's not always easy . . . when a man has to think about the needs of his wife and children. I know," he added, putting one hand to his forehead, "how difficult it can be."

Ezra gazed at his father as he continued to eat. He had never seen him quite like this before. He wondered if he had ever really known him. He felt as if his brain were too small to wrap itself around the things he'd been hearing. Could this really be what his father had been talking about all these years? Not rules and regulations and religious ceremonies, but wings and light and smoke and burning coals and flying creatures? And a God who really comes down and talks to people?

"Father," he said after a moment, "where does Mother go when she . . . goes out?"

Again the lines in Tola's face deepened. He shut his eyes and pinched the bridge of his nose between the thumb and forefinger of his right hand. His mouth hardened into a straight line. Ezra wondered if he were about to cry. He thought his father looked very much as if he were fighting back tears. Then, suddenly Tola braced himself, opened his eyes and looked up.

"That," he said to his son, "is something you'll have to ask *her*. Only she can answer that. But I can tell you this: The matters we discussed the other night—Ahaz and his flirtation with the foreign gods—are very serious indeed. Believe me, my son: Any man—or woman—who would play with strange fire must beware lest he—or she—be burned."

There it was again! That same old recurring refrain. Serious consequences. Strange fire. "Oh, come on, Father!" said Ezra. He could feel the hot flush rising in his cheeks. "You don't expect me to believe that about Mother, do you? What does it hurt if she goes out and has a little fun with . . . her friends?"

"I say nothing about your mother," answered Tola. "I only say this: The Lord is a jealous God! He will not accept second place. And as for the gods of the Syrians and the Assyrians—the Baals and Asherahs, and worst of all the Red King Molech," he paused and shuddered, "well, all I can tell you is that people do abominable things in their names. Abominable things as part of their worship."

"I don't believe it!" said Ezra. "King Ahaz may be an old grouch sometimes—and he does drink too much—but he's basically a good man. And he's done good things for the country. Mother says so. I can't picture him doing anything *abominable!*"

"Ezra," said Tola looking straight at his son, "has Hezekiah ever told you about his brothers?"

"Hezekiah doesn't have any brothers."

For a moment Tola bowed his head and held it between his hands. Then he looked up and said, "Ezra, the Red King is the bloody king of all the kings of the nations. Molech does not grant his favors for nothing. And so the kings of the earth make horrible offerings to him. Their own sons . . . they cause them to pass through the fire. Strange fire. Into the belly of the gruesome idol itself! I dare not speak of it further."

"No!" shouted Ezra jumping to his feet. "I don't believe any of that! King Ahaz wouldn't do such a thing. Mother wouldn't have anything to do with it. It's all just a story told by that fanatical prophet to turn people away from the new gods!"

And with that he threw down what was left of his bread and ran out into the street to look for Shub.

CHAPTER 6

No sooner had Ezra left his father's house than he was obliged to pass the circle of children who were playing wedding-and-funeral in the street. It was a very large circle by this time, for more than 20 children had joined the game, and it covered the narrow street from one side to the other. Ezra realized at once that he could not pass the circle at all, but would have to walk right through the middle of it if he wanted to get to the place where he thought Shub must be sitting with his harp—the base of a narrow flight of stone steps that connected Ezra's street with Mishneh Street up the hill. Ezra stopped, straightened his leather headband, and sighed. *Kids*, he thought. He would have preferred to avoid any contact with the neighborhood children this morning.

"Ezra!" shouted a round-faced little boy in a black-and-white-striped tunic. "Hey, it's Ezra! Come on, Ezra. Play with us."

Oh, great! thought Ezra. "Forget it, Jonathan," he yelled.

"Play us something, Gershom," called a petite girl in a brown robe.

Immediately an older boy in sheepskin began to play a tune on his wooden flute. It was a slow, sad air, set in a minor mode and filled with the haunting, empty spaces of the Judean wilderness beyond the city walls.

"Funeral!" shouted a dark-haired girl, jumping up and clapping her hands with excitement. At once the smile on her face gave way to a grim and piteous frown. She covered her head with a black shawl and began to parade around the edge of the circle with heavy, weary steps, wringing her hands and wailing as she went. The music droned on, and one by one the other children got to their feet and followed her example.

Ezra stood with folded arms, shifting his weight from one foot to the other. *This is ridiculous*, he thought. *I've got no time for kids' games today!*

"Come on, Ezra," called the little girl in the brown robe. "Funeral! Funeral! Come on."

Ignoring her, Ezra shoved his way past several of the "mourners" and started across the circle. But just as he got to the center of the open space, the tune changed, suddenly jumping to a higher key, dropping its sad half-tones, and shifting into a happy, bouncing dance rhythm. Most of the children caught the change immediately. The girls threw off their veils and began to spin and twirl on their toes. The boys lifted their hands into the air and hopped up and down.

"Wedding!" yelled several voices at once. "Wedding! Wedding!"

"You're out!" shouted the small boy in the black-and-white tunic, pointing at a pudgy, curly-headed girl who was still moving very slowly and had neglected to remove the shawl from her head. "You're out! Wedding! The funeral's over. You too, Ezra. You're out!"

Give me a break, thought Ezra in disgust. "Get out of my way," he snorted, glaring down at the boy and shoving him roughly aside. "I've got better things to do." Then he broke through the other side of the circle and took off running up the street.

He hadn't gone far—only a hundred paces or so to a narrow spot where the canyonlike street curved to the right—when another sound stopped him short. It was a sound that chilled him to the bone and made his hair stand on end, in spite of the bright morning light that streamed down over the tiled and wattled roofs of the houses. It was the sound of a voice. The voice of an old woman.

It was Old Hephzibah's voice.

"Alms! Alms!" cried white-haired Old Hephzibah from her seat on the stony gray doorstep of a house just beyond the bend in the street. Her arm was still in a sling of dirty brown wool, and she sat leaning on the end of a crooked walking staff of gnarled olivewood. "Alms for a poor old woman who can no longer work to support herself."

Ezra stood paralyzed. *This can't be happening. It's like I can't get away from the old witch!* A cold sweat broke out on his forehead. His hands and knees began to shake. He wasn't scared, he told himself—what was there to be scared of? But he *was* concerned about the success of his new strategy. He couldn't let her see him. It would spoil everything.

"Alms! Alms! Alms for a poor old widow with a broken arm!"

He had to get past her somehow. He had to link up with Shub and explain his plan for that night and get him to communicate it to Hezekiah. He looked around for some way of escape. The house on his right had an outdoor stairway. *That's it!* he thought.

Without a moment's hesitation he turned and ran. Up the steps he dashed as if pursued by Death itself. Gaining the roof of the house, he rushed across to the low parapet at the other side, and from there vaulted to the roof of the next house. *Lucky the houses are built so close together here*, he thought as he made his way across that roof as well and repeated the process. At the fifth house he found another outdoor stairway and descended to the street just at the spot where the lane of narrow stairs climbed the hill to Mishneh Street. Shub was right where he had expected to find him, sitting on the first step. Ezra breathed a sigh of relief as he ran over to greet his friend.

"Shub!" he called. But Shub did not hear him. There he sat, lost to the world, his precious *kinnor* cradled in the crook of his left arm, the fingers of his right hand deftly and speedily flying back and forth over the 10 gut strings, plucking out a swiftly flowing stream of chords and bright single notes. It was clear that Shub was deaf to everything but his own music. His head was back, his eyes closed, his thick black hair flying in every conceivable direction as he swayed in time to the melody. Then, as Ezra watched, Shub opened his mouth and began to sing:

I will sing for the one I love a song about his
    vineyard:
My loved one had a vineyard on a fertile
    hillside.
He dug it up and cleared it of stones and
    planted it with the choicest vines.
He built a watchtower in it and cut out a
    winepress as well.
Then he looked for a crop of good grapes, but
    it yielded only bad fruit. . . .

Ezra was entranced. He was no expert when it came to music, but somehow he felt that he'd never heard anything quite so lovely in all his life. The melody gripped him and held him. It was strong and sweet, distant and sad.

Now I will tell you what I am going to do to
    my vineyard:
I will take away its hedge, and it will be
    destroyed;
I will break down its wall, and it will be
    trampled.
I will make it a wasteland . . .

Ezra had never heard Shub sing before—poor, clumsy Shub. He had always known that Shub played the *kinnor*, but . . . such music! He rubbed his eyes. He couldn't believe that these sounds were coming from his friend's fingers and mouth.

> *The vineyard of the Lord Almighty is the*
> *house of Israel,*
> *and the men of Judah are the garden of his*
> *delight.*
> *And he looked for justice, but saw bloodshed;*
> *for righteousness, but heard cries of distress.*

The song ended as abruptly as it had begun. Shub let his right hand drop to his side. His chin fell onto his chest and he sat there for a moment, eyes closed. Stealthily, quietly, Ezra approached and laid a hand on his shoulder.

"Wedding!" said Ezra with a loud laugh.

Shub started violently and opened his eyes. Then, recognizing Ezra, he relaxed and smiled. "Actually," he said, "I'd say it's more funeral-like."

"But it's a love song—right?"

"Yes. About a lost love. It's a very sad song, really."

"Where'd you learn it? Is it yours?"

"Oh, no!" said Shub with a little self-deprecating laugh. "My father wrote it."

Your father? thought Ezra. He pictured the towering, daunting figure of Isaiah, the stern face framed in curling side locks and flowing gray-streaked beard. *That stuffy old goat writes songs like that?*

"Well," he said, straightening his headband and clearing his throat, "it was pretty good. Not bad at all, really."

"Thanks," said Shub, his cheeks coloring slightly.

"Yeah. But that's not why I came."

"Why, then?"

"Shub, your father knows about these things. Where do we go to find a . . . Molech festival?"

"Molech? Are you crazy?"

"No. This is important, Shub! I want you and Hezekiah and my father—especially my father—to see. We went to the high place last night and nothing bad happened. We can go to the altar of Molech, too. That'll really show 'em!"

"But Ezra, do you know what happens there?"

Ezra laughed. "Oh, sure. My father tried to scare me with all those stories. Now do you know how to get there?"

"Well," Shub answered slowly, leaning his cheek against the curve of his harp and caressing the strings, "I've *heard* that it's outside the city. In the Hinnom Valley, South—through the Potsherd Gate, on a little rise of hilly ground under a big terebinth tree."

"Good. You get Hezekiah and meet me right here after dark. Bring your *kinnor* and be ready for a *really* good time!"

"But Ezra, I—"

"Listen, Shub. Are you my friend or not?"

"Of course I am."

"And are you as sick as I am of all this Remnant stuff—this business of keeping up our *fathers'* reputations at the expense of our own lives?"

"Well, sure. You know I am."

"All right then. Bring Hezekiah. You'll see. They'll *all* see! Nothing bad will happen. And then they won't be able to say another word about it. Ever."

CHAPTER 7

That afternoon Ezra fell asleep over his lessons. It could have happened to anyone. Mishael, the scribe who tutored Ezra and six other boys in one of the small priestly chambers off the temple courtyard, was about as dull as a teacher could possibly be. He was a thin little man with a gray beard, curling white earlocks, and a long, pointed nose that stuck out prominently beyond the shadow of the blue-bordered shawl with which he covered his pious head. Ever and always his voice droned on and on in the same midrange monotone as he lectured at great length about the Levitical prescriptions for the cleansing of lepers or the proper way to execute the serif on the letter *zayin*.

Under Mishael's hypnotic influence, in the dark coolness of the stone-walled chamber, Ezra could have easily dropped off almost anytime. And today he was seriously short on sleep as a result of the previous night's escapade. All through the first part of the lesson his eyes drooped like lead and the yawns came thick and fast. When the scribe's back was turned and the other boys were busy practicing their letters with stylus and clay palette, Ezra took the opportunity to close his eyes and rest his head in his hands—just for a moment or two.

But how strange! No sooner had he bowed his head than it seemed to him that a thin, high string of harp notes floated into the room and began falling on the paving stones like sparkling drops of rain.

Shub? thought Ezra. But no, it couldn't be. Shub couldn't possibly be there. Shub's father gave him his lessons at home. And yet the sound of his friend's *kinnor* was unmistakable. Even more unmistakable was the clear tone of Shub's voice as the harp notes blended with the words of the song:

> *What more could have been done for my*
> *vineyard than I have done for it?*
> *When I looked for good grapes, why did it*
> *yield only bad?*

Ezra lifted his head and looked around the room for Shub. Nowhere could he see the tall, gangly form of his friend. But what he *did* see caused him to open his mouth and gape in disbelief.

Wings. The whole place was full of wings. Transparent wings. Transparent faces, too: some smiling, some stern, some etched with pain, others flaming with fiery indignation. They all seemed to be made of billowing smoke and flowing, liquid light, so that Ezra could glimpse the forms of Mishael and his fellow students right through them. And up near the ceiling, in the right front corner of the room, was a blinding, luminous blaze, like the eye of the sun, and what looked like great convoluted folds of a large sheet of gold cloth pouring down out the heart of it and onto the schoolroom floor.

And he looked for justice, but saw bloodshed;
for righteousness, but heard cries of distress.

On and on the voice sang, changing gradually as the song progressed. Now it was the voice of his father, now of the prophet Isaiah. Now it was his mother's voice, sweet and melodic as a cooing dove's, but faint and fading into the distance. Then it became the voice of Shub's brother, Maher-Shalal-Hash-Baz, whose pudgy, fuzz-topped face leered down at Ezra from among the other faces and wings, taunting, accusing, warbling a tattletale singsong.

Ezra tore his eyes away from the face of the nine-year-old junior prophet and focused them on Mishael's back. As he did so, the music of the song slowly deteriorated and faded into the scribe's dry monotone. Then, as he watched, his teacher turned and began walking straight toward him, his long-nosed face perfectly hidden within the shadow of his scribal head covering.

"For righteousness," droned Mishael's voice. "For righteousness. He looked for righteousness, but heard cries of distress."

Ezra cringed as the man drew near and bent over him. The spindly little scribe stopped, drew back the veil from his face and—it was the face of Old Hephzibah! She reached out with her one good arm and aimed a bony finger straight at Ezra.

"Who will go?" she demanded in her high, creaking voice. "Whom shall we send? Who will go for us? Is it you? You young ruffian! Is it you? Is it *you?*"

"No!" shouted Ezra. "No! Not me!"

"Who will show us the correct way to write the letter *tsadhe?*" droned the voice of his teacher. "Will you, Ezra?"

"No! No!" Ezra screamed, jumping up from

the place where he had been sitting on the cool stone floor. "Not me!"

Mishael leaned over him with a puzzled look in his eyes and a single drop of sweat glistening on the end of his pointed nose. "Ezra! What in the name of Zion is *wrong* with you?"

"N-nothing," answered Ezra. He glanced around and saw that the other boys were all laughing at him. "I-I'm sick, teacher, that's all. Awful sick!" He groaned to strengthen his case. "I think I better go home!"

"I suppose you'd better," said Mishael in a distressed tone, backing away from his student with a look of alarm.

Ezra got up in a daze and stumbled out the door.

CHAPTER 8

As soon as Tola learned of his son's strange and sudden sickness, for Mishael had lost no time in reporting it to him, he confined Ezra to his room for the rest of the afternoon and evening. It was unthinkable, he explained, that a boy so seriously ill should leave his bed until a qualified physician or man of God had had a chance to examine him. He even hinted that he might ask the prophet Isaiah himself to make a house call. At this suggestion, Ezra perked up and insisted that he was feeling much better. But Tola was unrelenting. Ezra was not to leave his room until the hour of his lessons the following day at the earliest.

There was no supper to speak of that night—just more of the same round loaves and *leben* he had shared with his father that morning. Jehudith had gone out again.

Ezra ate his meager meal alone and in silence, sitting on his reed sleeping mat as the last slanting rays of the red sun faded from his window. Tola's measures were seriously complicating his plans to meet Shub and Hezekiah at the base of the stone stairway after dark. But he hadn't given up hope. This wasn't anything he couldn't handle. *I can still sneak out the door after Father goes to bed*, he told himself.

But then he found out that the door was going to be blocked that night—blocked in a most unexpected and frustrating way. Apparently Tola had invited a houseguest to come and sleep in the front entry hall—the last houseguest Ezra would *ever* have chosen to sleep under the same roof with him.

"Old Hephzibah," he whined when his father told him. "You can't be serious!"

"It's the least we can do for her, Ezra," Tola responded. "She's old. She's a widow. And now that she's hurt her arm, she can't possibly fend for herself. If there's one thing I've learned from the prophet, it's that the Lord wants us to look out for people like Old Hephzibah. Isaiah has said it many times:

> *Defend the cause of the fatherless, plead the*
> *case of the widow.*
> *Provide the poor wanderer with shelter.*

Then your light will break forth like the dawn.
Then your righteousness will go before you.

"I really don't think we have any choice except to take her in."

That absolutely settled it. Rendezvous or no rendezvous, there was no way Ezra was going to wait around that house for a confrontation with Old Hephzibah. He just *had* to get out. So as soon as his father left the room, he grabbed his cloak and took the only way of escape that was left to him.

Off came the lattice. Up onto the sill went Ezra. Then, leaning out the window as far as he could, he laid hold of the nearest branch of the almond tree that grew outside and swung himself out. The scent of the almond blossoms invaded his nostrils. The gentle night breeze brushed his cheek. He was out; he was free! It was great to be alive.

He found the others waiting for him at the bottom of the stairway leading to Mishneh Street. Shub was there with his precious *kinnor*. Hezekiah had covered himself in the same ragged, ash-smeared sackcloth robe he had worn the previous evening. Overhead, the first stars were gleaming dully through a gauzy veil of gathering cloud and mist. Ezra took a deep breath and straightened his headband. This was going to be his night of nights. The making of a true hero.

"Well," he said, spreading his feet and folding his arms, "I'd say it's time we got going. What do you guys say?"

Hezekiah got up from the step where he was sitting, glanced at the sky, and drew his cloak closer around his shoulders. "Where are you taking us this time?"

"Didn't Shub tell you?"

Hezekiah looked at Shub. Shub shrugged his shoulders. "No, Shub didn't tell me. As a matter of fact, he's been acting pretty funny about the whole thing. I almost didn't come. I figured you must be up to something *really* bad this time. You're *going* to get caught one of these days, Ezra, and I don't know if I want to be around when it happens."

Ezra laughed. "So what if I do? What's it to you? And anyway, you *did* come—which shows that you *know* I'm right after all."

"I don't know about that." Hezekiah bit his lip, rubbed his right temple, and sat down on the step again. "I'm not sure *why* I came. I guess there are some things I have to find out for myself."

"Whatever," said Ezra impatiently. "So do you

still want to know where we're going?"

Hezekiah looked up. "I've got an idea, but . . . go ahead and tell me."

"All right, then." Ezra drew himself up to his full height, pushed the dark curls out of his face, and smiled. "We're going to a *Molech* festival."

Shub shuddered at the name of the Red King. Hezekiah set his jaw, folded his hands in his lap, and stared down at them. "I had a feeling you'd say that," he said.

"So are you still coming?" Ezra asked.

Hezekiah didn't answer right away. He just bit his lip and kept staring down at his two thumbs where they lay locked in his lap. His face was pale and his eyes looked glassy. Ezra stared at him and shifted his weight from one foot to the other. He felt very uncomfortable for some reason. *That Hezekiah. Scared and worried again.* It was the same old story. And yet, somehow, there was something different about it this time. *Well, he can go on home if he wants to*, Ezra told himself. *I've had just about enough of his worrying anyhow.*

"I don't *want* to go," Hezekiah said at last. "But . . . but maybe I *should*."

Shub perked up at this. "Should?" he said. "What do you mean *should*?"

"I need to know," Hezekiah said slowly, ". . . exactly what happened to them."

"Them?" Ezra shot a questioning glance at Shub. Shub looked down at his *kinnor*.

"I've only heard rumors," Hezekiah continued. "I asked my mother several times before she died. But she wouldn't talk to me about it. Sometimes I think that's what killed her—the grief and the shame . . . and the fear. Not that they were *her* sons. They were the children of other wives. But she was afraid.

"Shub's father says I'm under Yahweh's special protection. Otherwise, the same thing would have happened to *me*. Supposedly Isaiah made a big deal of it in his prophecies when I was born. There was an oracle or something."

"Yes," said Shub quietly, without looking up.

For to us a child is born, to us a son is given,
and the government will be on his
shoulders. . . .
He will reign on David's throne and over his
kingdom, establishing and upholding it
with justice and righteousness . . .

Ezra was confused. "What are you guys talking about?"

"I'm going to sit on my father's throne someday," Hezekiah went on, ignoring Ezra's question. His lip was beginning to tremble. "And yet, by right, it should have gone to one of *them*. I just have to find out what . . . *happened* to them. I don't really want to know, but I *need* to know." He looked up into Ezra's eyes. "Do you understand?"

"No," said Ezra angrily. "I *don't* understand! And I'm not going to take the time to try right now. You're wasting my time. If we don't get going soon it'll be too late! Do you know the way, Shub?"

Shub stood up and gave him a sheepish look. "I think so," he said.

"Well, then—lead on!"

CHAPTER 9

This night's walk was even darker and more unsettling than the journey the boys had made to Ophel the night before. There was no moon—Ezra knew that it would rise a little later on—and clouds were rapidly blocking out what little light fell from the stars. They encountered no one as they picked their way along through the somber alleys and lanes of Jerusalem, staying close to the walls of the shops and houses. Mishneh Street was quiet. Even the cramped and winding lane that led past Ophel, through *Ha'iyr David*, and eventually to the Potsherd Gate was strangely empty: no beggars, no thieves, no painted women veiled in red. The air felt close and heavy, and a sense of unspoken threat hung in the atmosphere. Ezra and his friends barely said three words to one another until they were outside the city.

Luckily, they did not need to get past a sentry in order to make their exit. Hezekiah knew how to get out without using the Potsherd Gate at all: through a small, unwatched portal between the two walls near the King's Garden—a place known only to the royal family and their retainers.

Once beyond the walls, the boys made a sharp turn to the right and began their descent into the Hinnom Valley. On this particular night, *Gey' Hinnom* looked every bit as deep and dark as its reputation. At least Ezra thought so. He had often heard about the mysterious, forbidden things that went on in this place during the hours after sunset: secret pagan rites, wild dances, unspeakable sacrifices. He shivered a little as he thought about it—not because he was afraid, he told himself, but out of excitement.

Hinnom's sides were steep and rocky. The boys did not reach the bottom without stubbing their sandaled toes and falling and scraping their knees often. Shub, of course, fell at least five times as much as the other two. And yet, somehow, he managed to keep his precious harp from getting a single scratch.

Once at the bottom of the ravine, Ezra called a halt and looked around. The night had grown exceptionally dark. It was difficult to see their way. But down toward the west end of the valley Ezra could see the reddish glow of a faint and eerie light. It throbbed and pulsed against the underside of the gathering clouds and what looked like a column of rising smoke.

"This way," he said, gathering his cloak around him with one hand and pointing at the glow with the other. "We're on the right track!"

"Are we?" asked Hezekiah in a doubtful tone, dragging his feet as the older boys led the way. Shub pulled his *kinnor* deeper into the folds of his cloak and trudged ahead beside the intrepid Ezra.

Patiently, doggedly they followed the glowing column of smoke until they came to a place where the ground began to rise in a gentle upward slope. They paused at the base of a small, round-topped hill.

"What's this?" asked Hezekiah, squinting through the darkness and reaching out to touch the top of what appeared to be a leafy hedge.

"Grapevines," answered Shub. "It's a vineyard. Looks like there's a garden just beyond the rows, too. Father says they always put these places in the middle of gardens and under big, spreading trees. Gardens are sacred—'holy'—to Molech worshipers."

Ezra could see that the reddish smoke was rising from the top of the hill. Obviously, this was another *bamah,* or high place. Faintly, through the darkness, he could hear the confused noise of jumbled voices and a few rumbling drums and tinkling bells. He straightened his headband and set his jaw. "What are we waiting for?" he said. "Let's get going!"

They pushed their way past the vines and up through terraced beds of flax, coriander, and rue—flowers that would have danced with bright color under the sunlight, but only gleamed dull and gray in the darkness. Up the slope they labored, breathing heavily, always keeping the forbidding vision of luminescent smoke before their faces. Behind him, Ezra could hear Shub chanting lines of verse to himself in a low, thoughtful voice:

> *You will be disgraced because of the gardens*
> *that you have chosen.*
> *You will be like an oak with fading leaves,*
> *like a garden without water.*

As for Ezra, the words of another song were pounding through *his* head. Try as he might, he simply could not get rid of them:

> *Now I will tell you what I am going to do to*
> *my vineyard:*
> *I will take away its hedge, and it will be*
> *destroyed;*

*I will break down its wall, and it will be
trampled.*

Over and over again those words sang themselves to him. The farther up the slope he climbed,
the more maddening it became. He felt that he
must find some way to stop it. In a moment or
two he'd have no choice. He'd have to scream or
throw something or turn and run back down the
hill. Anything to banish that song from his
thoughts!

That's when they reached the summit.

Ezra put out a hand and signaled the others to
halt. Before them lay a wide circle of ruddy light.
The boys stopped just beyond its margin and
stared. The scene in front of them was similar to
the one they had witnessed at Ophel the night before. And yet it was different, too—different in
some indefinably chilling way, Ezra thought. He
shivered again and told himself that the night air
was growing colder.

In the center of the open space on the hilltop
stood a terebinth tree. Ezra knew that it must be
very old. He had never seen a terebinth so tall or
with such thick and widely spreading branches. A
flickering red-orange light played over the bark of
its gnarled trunk and skipped through the open

spaces in the overarching ceiling of its lance-shaped leaves.

Below the tree was the source of the pulsating light: a towering altar of baked brick standing at the top of a flight of 10 wide steps. It was topped by a stone image of the Red King himself—the head of a bull on a grotesquely distorted human figure squatting on its haunches. Within its bowels danced the flames of a fierce and roaring fire. The idol's apelike arms were outstretched as if to receive the offerings of its worshipers. Even at this distance Ezra could tell that the statue was hollow and that any object placed in its arms would roll instantly down through its tubelike body and into the raging flames below.

"So," said Hezekiah quietly, almost to himself. "*That's* what he looks like." Shub gave a low whistle.

"Let's see if we can get any closer," urged Ezra. He was surprised at the hoarse, dry sound of his own voice.

As the boys inched forward, they could see that the people gathered around the altar—a much smaller crowd than the one at Ophel—were divided into two groups.

On the left hand stood the women. Some were veiled and solemn. Others looked wild and disheveled. A few were wailing and chanting in strange, high voices, their dark robes loose and open, their faces streaked with paint. Several of these robes were of a pattern strangely familiar to Ezra: midnight blue, with a stripe of Tyrian purple at the hem.

Suddenly a thought occurred to him: *Could Mother be here?* At once his heart began to pound. His eyes roved back and forth in search of her. What if she *were* here? With Hanun? But it was no use. In the throbbing half-light it was impossible to get a good look at any of the faces.

On the right side stood the men. Some were heavily cloaked, their faces covered. Others were bare-chested. A group of them held musical instruments—lyres, pipes, drums, or cymbals. And a few, oddly enough, carried babies in their arms. As the boys watched and listened, the drums took up a hypnotic beat. The infants started to scream.

"Babies!" whispered Hezekiah, gripping Ezra tightly by the arm. "It's what I was afraid of. I asked them, over and over, but no one would ever talk to me about it!"

"Quiet!" hissed Ezra angrily. He didn't want to think about Hezekiah's problems. The thought of his mother being there with Hanun was proving even harder to banish than the words to Shub's song. For the first time he asked himself whether it had been a good idea to come.

Between the men and the women, directly in front of the altar, stood a tall figure in a flowing scarlet robe. As the boys watched, this man walked over to a bronze pot that hung from a tripod over a small cooking fire. Leaning over the pot, he dipped a ladle into it and poured a measure of steaming red broth—what it was made of, Ezra could not guess—into a wooden bowl. Then, taking a step forward, he raised the bowl in both hands and called out in a loud voice: "Keep to yourselves! Do not come near me, for I am holier than you!" With that he put the bowl to his lips and drank deeply.

"Holier! Holier! Holier than we!" chanted the people. The cymbals chimed and the drums pounded.

"Let the circle be cast!" called the man in red. "Let the dance begin!"

At his words the entire group fanned out and formed itself into a wide ring. Instantly the beating of the drums grew louder. The pipes and lyres intoned a dark, alluring tune in a mysterious, ancient mode. Slowly the feet of the celebrants began moving in time to the music, at first with carefully measured steps, then with increasing agitation as the melody line rose and dipped and rose again. The pounding of the drums grew more insistent. The drone of the pipes swelled.

Ezra shook himself. Was this, after all, just another dream? His foot was tapping to the rhythm of the music; he couldn't remember when it had started. It seemed to him that it had always been tapping. He felt that his mind was emptying itself, like a pitcher of water poured out on the sand. He pinched himself and fought to control his thoughts. "Mother," he whispered, casting his eyes around the moving circle. He *had* to know if she was there. Without thinking, he stepped into the light and made a move to join the dancers.

Shub was at his side in an instant, his *kinnor* nestled securely in the crook of his left arm, the fingers of his right hand already plucking the tune in unison with the other instruments. Ezra turned to look at his face and saw the red light of the flames reflected in his eyes.

"This is why I came!" said Shub in an excited tone of voice Ezra had never heard him use before. "To play. Maybe all night long. With real musicians!" And with that he broke away from his friends and ran to join the other lyrists and pipers.

Through the gathering fog in his mind, Ezra somehow became dimly aware that Shub was not acting like himself. Something, he felt, was wrong with Shub. He blinked and tried to swallow, but his throat was too dry. Something was wrong with this whole situation—dreadfully wrong. Dizziness threatened to overwhelm him, but he fought it off. *Dance*, he thought vaguely. *I've got to join the dance.*

He turned to Hezekiah who was lagging behind and looking for a chance to slip away. "Come on," he said in a voice that sounded as if it belonged to someone else. "Let's go! Nothing bad will happen. You'll see." And then he grabbed Hezekiah by the arm and pulled him into the circle.

Why did I say that? The question drifted into his mind as if from a distance as he and Hezekiah were swept away with the furious beat of the drums, the swirl of the dancers' robes, and the high, skirling wail of the flutes and pipes and vibrating strings. *Why am I doing this? This isn't right. Something bad is going to happen, I just know it.* But it was too late to stop now. Ezra felt his brain relax and let go, like an overstrained muscle. He ceased to think.

How long they were caught in the whirling maelstrom of the circle he did not know. On and on it turned, like the relentless turning of the starry sky-wheel, like an irresistible sucking vortex in the heart of the sea. The music swelled and the red light of the flames flashed past his eyes over and over again.

And then—without warning—there was a face. A cry of distress, a dark hood thrown back, and a weary, bearded face, etched with deep lines, emerging from the swirling storm of light and dark and revolving colors. A face open-mouthed, staring-eyed, wearing an expression of confusion and fear. A face that was looking not at Ezra but at someone beside him.

"Hezekiah!" cried the voice that burst from the mouth in the face. "Hezekiah! What are *you* doing here?"

It was King Ahaz.

CHAPTER 10

At that cry everything came to a halt. The circle slowed and stopped. The chanting ceased. The dancers turned and gaped at the king. The music dragged, hesitated, soured, and fell apart. The wailing infants grew quiet. From across the circle Ezra caught a glimpse of Shub's face, pale and wide-eyed as if he had just snapped out of a nightmare. Slowly the prophet's son lowered his harp and stared.

In the silence that followed, Ezra saw the man in red come striding across the open space toward them. Bells tinkled at the hem of his voluminous robe, and bright rings flashed on his long fingers. The features of his face, as grim and severe as if they were chiseled from stone, lurked threateningly within the shadows of his scarlet head-covering. On he came, with a slow and stately step, until he stood beside the king. There he stopped and smiled thinly down at Hezekiah.

"Your son?" he said, glancing sideways at the king. "Well! I think it is fairly clear what he is doing here. The Red King has drawn him. For a purpose."

Ezra could see that Ahaz was shaken. The great talker, the easy conversationalist, the social charmer, the persuasive leader—this is how Ezra had always thought of his king. Now he saw him as someone a lot like himself: small, shivering, frightened, vulnerable. Quickly his eyes moved from the king's face to the face of the man in red, and then to the dark, overclouded face of the sky above. From beyond Hinnom's western rim the sound of distant thunder reached his ears.

"What are you saying, Tammuz . . . great priest?" asked Ahaz. He barely moved his cracked, dry lips as he spoke. Sweat ran in two trickling streams down his cheeks.

"I say nothing," answered the priest of Molech. "The great Red King speaks for himself. Can't you hear him? Isn't his will plain to all who have eyes to see and ears to hear?"

A low murmur ran around the circle. Ahaz turned a pale face upon his son and said nothing. Ezra saw the pleading look in Hezekiah's eyes as he returned his father's glance.

"Weren't we speaking of this very thing tonight, just before we called the circle together?" the priest persisted. "Haven't you confided to many of your advisors and closest friends your firm belief that only the power of Molech can remove the Assyrian's thumb from the small of Judah's back? As in the past, so it will be on this occasion. By the hand of the Red King we may yet fight fire with fire."

More voices. Another rumble in the sky. And close at hand, one of the Molech worshipers suddenly spoke. "He is right, Your Majesty. We discussed this subject at your dinner party the other night. You remember. We agreed then that Assyrian gods might very well be the key to ridding us of the Assyrians . . . and their tribute. You said so yourself."

That voice, thought Ezra. A sick thrill of recognition coursed through his brain and body as it rang in his ears. He turned to see the darkly handsome face, framed by a black beard. Hanun. *Him again!* If Hanun were there, could his mother be there too? Once more he scanned the circle in search of her face, but to no avail.

"It is true," King Ahaz was saying. Sweat poured down his face. His eyes were fixed on the ground. "I did say it. But *this*," he added, looking up at the priest, "I never meant to go through *this* again!"

"Ahaz," said Tammuz in calm, measured tones, "it is clear to me that Meni, the Lord of Destiny, and Molech, the Red King, have joined counsel this night. The sacrifice has been provided. Yes! Provided by the hand of Molech, that the power of Molech might be released!"

With that the priest laid one hand on Hezekiah's shoulder. With the other he beckoned to two dark-robed men who stood several paces away, awaiting his orders.

"Bind the boy!" he called. "Let him be prepared. He goes to join his brothers. He goes to the great Red King. It is the will of Molech!"

"*Molech! Molech!*" chanted the circle of worshipers.

"Now stand away!" shouted Tammuz with a flourish as the men in the dark cloaks drew near. Just beyond them Ezra could see Shub, his *kinnor* under his arm and an alarmed expression on his face. In the next moment the prophet's son began to cross the open space at a run.

"Away! Keep to yourselves!" the priest shouted, his arms raised above his head, the huge sleeves of his red robe falling down around his shoulders. "Do not come near, for I am holier than you!"

"Holier! Holier! Holier than we!" echoed the crowd.

"And this boy—this prince of Judah—he is holier than all. He goes to the Red King!"

"The Red King!"

Shub ran up to Ezra, panic in his face. Ezra shot him a questioning glance, then looked over at Hezekiah, who was visibly trembling.

"Let the circle be extended!" cried the priest, his voice growing louder and more frenzied with every word. Each worshiper took three steps backward. "Wider and wider. Until there is room for all the gods and all the forces of the high and circling wheel of heaven. Sun and moon and stars. Call upon them, one and all, to attend us! Let there be no narrowing of the circle. Let their power be joined to the power of the Red King. Let them come and serve us in exchange for the sacrifice we offer!"

"Ezra," pleaded Shub in an urgent whisper, "you see what's happening! Do something!"

Ezra felt as if he were about to faint. "*Me?*" he said. "*Me* do something? What can *I* do?"

There was no time to think clearly. The dark-robed men were only a few steps away. Already their sinewy arms were outstretched to lay hold of Hezekiah. Hardly knowing what he was doing, Ezra grabbed the prince by the edge of his sackcloth cloak.

"Run, Hezekiah!" he shouted.

Then, dragging his friend after him, Ezra turned and fled.

"I'm right behind you!" shouted Shub.

This bold move took the priest and his men by surprise. The boys were several strides beyond the circle before they heard any noise of pursuit. Then a great outcry rose at their backs, followed by a flash of lightning and another peal of crackling thunder.

Ezra ran, conscious only of the wildly elongated and leaping shadows that the altar's flames cast before him. Dimly, just ahead, he could discern the gray patches and rows of the terraced garden beds along the descending slope. Behind him he could hear Shub's labored breathing and the pounding of his heavy footsteps. It seemed to him that the noise of the crowd and the shouts of their pursuers were fading. A thrill of hope shot through him. *We're going to make it*, he thought. *We're going to make it!*

Then, just as it looked as if the rows of grapevines were within their reach—*crash!*

"*Mmmpphh!*"

A burst of sounds just at Ezra's back: a sickening thud; a muffled cry; the crunching of wood and the jangling of snapping strings. *Shub*, he thought. *That clumsy Shub. He's tripped and fallen again!*

A nauseated feeling rising in the pit of his stomach, Ezra slowed his steps and turned to look for his friend. Instantly pain shot down his arm as strong hands grasped and held him. He heard Hezekiah cry out in anguish.

"Ezra," whimpered Shub as two large men yanked him to his feet. "My *kinnor!* It's ruined! Oh, we should never have come."

In a matter of moments all three boys stood once again in the flickering light of the altar, facing the king and the priest.

Ahaz had no indulgent smile for them this time. He avoided their eyes. He drew his cloak around his shoulders and stared down at his feet. At last he muttered, "I am sorry . . . my son. It seems there is no other way. Apparently it is the god's will."

"Even so," assented Tammuz. "Now take him! Let him be brought near. The Red King calls!"

"No!" screamed Ezra, his eyes darkening with despair as two black-robed men stooped to bind the prince. "Hezekiah, I never meant for this to happen!"

Hezekiah turned to face his friend. He said nothing.

"It can't happen. Not to *you!*" cried Ezra as the men tightened the knots of the cords. Then a crazy idea popped into his head. It had worked before; maybe it would work again. "Take me!" he shouted. "Take me instead. It's my fault, Your Majesty. Let them take *me* instead!"

"I'm sorry," mumbled the king, still without looking up. "It cannot be."

"The Red King demands a king's son," said the priest, who stood beside Ahaz with folded arms. "No other will do."

Ezra's knees felt like rubber. His face was hot and feverish. *I've got to stop this somehow*, he thought. Suddenly he remembered something.

"But Hezekiah," he said, laying a hand on his friend's shoulder as the men began to pull the prince in the direction of the altar, "what about Isaiah's prophecy? What about the promise that Yahweh will protect you and make you sit on your father's throne?"

"I don't know," said the prince. "He must have been talking about someone else. There must be another."

Then the men dragged them apart. Ezra watched helplessly as his friend, in the company of the scarlet-robed priest, was led across the open circle to the base of the brick stairway that led to the altar.

CHAPTER 11

"Wait!" screamed Ezra, shocked at the sound of his own voice. So loud, so urgent was its tone that every eye in that horrible circle, every face, etched in flickering lines of black and red by the light of the flames, turned toward him.

The priest raised a hand and stopped the men on the bottom step of the great stone altar. The bells on the fringes of his long scarlet robe jangled; the gold and silver rings on his fingers flashed in the firelight as he turned, put his hands on his hips, and glared at Ezra. Ezra could see the whites of the man's eyes, shining like two milky crescent moons in the night of his dark and frowning face. They fixed the beam of their stare upon him through the lurid, smoky air. "*Another* interruption! What do you mean by it, impudent boy?" the priest demanded.

Ezra found himself striding boldly into the center of the circle. He straightened his headband, planted his feet, and raised his arms toward the sky. "In the name of all that is holy," he called out in a loud voice, "I ask leave to speak with the king!"

A murmur ran from one end of the open space to the other—a murmur that seemed to find an echo in the stirring of the leaves as the wind sighed through the branches of the great terebinth tree. From the lowering sky above came another rumble of thunder. The priest scowled. He was opening his mouth to say something when suddenly Ahaz stepped up to him.

"Let the boy speak, Tammuz," the king commanded. The priest of Molech hesitated, raised one hand, and opened his mouth. Then, as if thinking better of whatever he had planned to say, he folded his hands, bowed, and took a step backward.

Ezra was trembling violently. He felt sure everyone could see him shake. Any moment, he feared, his knees would begin knocking together uncontrollably and his teeth would start chattering. His throat tightened, causing him to gasp for air. He was terribly afraid and he knew it. But he also knew that, for just this once, he was doing the right thing and dared not stop.

"O King," he said, his voice quavering painfully, "I—I think you're making a terrible mistake."

The murmur rose again, louder this time. Ezra ignored it and pushed ahead. "Yes!" he said, gathering confidence. "A huge mistake. Don't you see? You're playing right into a trap!"

The murmur became an excited babble. The priest took a step toward Ahaz, his face twisted into an expression of outrage. The king put out a hand and held him off.

"Go on, boy," said Ahaz, moving closer to Ezra, his face pale and wet but strangely eager, his lip trembling. "What trap? What do you mean?"

"Well," answered Ezra, stretching the moment of advantage, "it's like this: You're asking a foreign god to help you get rid of the foreigners. Does that make sense?"

Ahaz said nothing, but an odd kind of light seemed to dawn in his haggard face.

"It seems to me," continued Ezra, "that once a god like this Molech sees you bowing down at his altar, he's got you right where he wants you. And that can't be good, because . . . well, after all, he's on *their* side—the Assyrians, I mean. What then? I'll tell you: *Wham! Bam!* He calls in his people to finish you off! Old Tiglath Pileser, King of Assyria, couldn't have come up with a better plan himself."

More murmurs and another growl of thunder, but the king didn't seem to hear any of it. He was leaning closer and closer to Ezra, listening intently, his hands clasped tightly together.

"Besides," Ezra went on hesitantly, "Israel—and Judah—have their own God. Right? Isn't our own God strong enough to take care of us? Why do we need Molech?"

"*Aaaagggghh!*" shrieked a woman somewhere on the edge of the circle. "This boy is one of *them!* He violates all that is holy. He narrows the great circle!"

"Exactly!" shouted the priest, his red robe swirling menacingly in the dancing light as he put out a hand to lay hold of the king's cloak. But once again Ahaz waved him back.

"Let the boy speak, I say!" shouted the king.

Ezra did. "And that's not all," he said. His stomach was churning. The hair above his leather headband was dripping with sweat. He licked his lips and tasted salt. He felt that he was coming to the point—the point of everything. "Israel's God says that what you're doing here is *wrong!*" He spoke the words, but could hardly believe that they were coming out of his own mouth. The circle burst into a chaotic outcry.

Out of the corner of his eye Ezra stole a glance

at Shub. The tall boy's mouth had dropped open so that his chin almost rested on his chest.

"Yes!" shouted Ezra. "It's wrong of you to kill your own son like this, King Ahaz! Israel's God calls that murder. He's not like the other gods. He'd never even *dream* of asking you to do something like this. He calls it an *abomination!* That's what my father says—and Shub's father, too, the prophet Isaiah. Israel's God promises to take care of you if you trust Him. But if you do this thing, you'll live to regret it. You'll have to face the consequences."

"Now he quotes Isaiah," laughed the woman in the circle. "The man no one believes!" Other voices mumbled assent.

Ezra looked straight at Ahaz, awaiting his response. He half expected the king to lash out at him in fury, to order his arrest, to cast him into the flames within the idol's belly along with Hezekiah. But Ahaz did none of those things. What he *did* was something Ezra could never have predicted. He dropped to his knees, covered his face with his hands, and began to weep uncontrollably. Somehow the sight struck fear into Ezra's heart—a far greater fear than any threat of punishment could have inspired.

"Seize the unholy blasphemer!" shouted the

priest of Molech pointing at Ezra, his dark countenance darker than ever with rage. But at that moment King Ahaz, in a sudden burst of unexpected and quite uncharacteristic energy, jumped to his feet and faced the man. Another peal of thunder, louder than any that had preceded it, burst from the heavens.

"No!" cried Ahaz, his jaw set, his face still wet with tears. "The boy is right. I *have* lived to regret it! Night after night, in the dark watches of the early morning hours, their faces have passed before me in a ghastly parade. I have regretted it over and over again, I tell you. But this time I say *no!*" Then he turned and called to the men who were holding Hezekiah on the bottom step of the altar. "Release my son! Your king commands it!"

Immediately the two dark-robed figures obeyed. Ezra caught the glint of polished bronze as they drew long, bright knives from somewhere within their cloaks. Every face in the circle turned toward the three figures who stood silhouetted against the pulsing orange glow of the furnace. The knives flashed, the ropes fell, and Hezekiah came dashing over to Ezra and his father where they stood in the middle of the circle.

"Now go, my son!" said Ahaz hoarsely. The king's face was deathly pale and creased with deep lines and furrows. "All of you boys go! Run! Back to the city as quickly as you can. And tell no one what you've seen!"

Ezra looked at Hezekiah. It seemed to him that his friend was too overwhelmed to move or speak. He stood staring up at his father out of great round eyes, as if seeing the man for the first time in his life. A few big drops of rain fell on the prince's forehead and dripped down his cheeks.

"Come on, Hezekiah!" said Ezra, grabbing his friend by the sleeve of his garment. "We'd better do as he says." He pulled the prince to the edge of the circle where Shub stood waiting. The other celebrants parted ranks to let them pass. Then, side by side, each one trembling from head to toe, the boys slowly began walking out of the range of the firelight, out of the great circle, up the slope of the Hinnom Valley toward the lights of Jerusalem that twinkled faintly through the falling rain.

"Stop!" boomed the priest. So loud and powerful was his voice that Ezra felt he had no choice except to obey. He stopped, turned, and saw the huge man throw back the hood of his cloak, revealing a wrinkled head, shaven in front and tattooed with dreadful symbols and signs—crescent moons, serpents, and spider webs. The priest grasped the king, who stood bent over and shaking, by the shoulders and cried out, "In the name of Molech, the great Red King, and of all that is holy, I tell you that you must complete the sacrifice or suffer destruction at the hands of the god. Seize the prince and bring him back!"

In answer to the priest's cry, several men broke from the circle and charged after the boys. At that very moment the rain suddenly began to pour from the sky in sheets. Then came a deafening crash of thunder and an explosion of lightning directly overhead. In the split second of illumination that followed, Ezra saw the altar of Molech enveloped in clouds of white smoke and boiling steam as the torrential rain drenched the altar and put out the fire within the idol's belly. Terrified, the priest's servants fell to the ground or ran for their lives.

"What are we waiting for?" Ezra shouted to his two friends. "Let's get out of here!"

And then the three boys turned and ran toward the city with all their strength.

CHAPTER 12

She isn't coming home."

Ezra winced at his father's words. He sat at the end of his sleeping pallet hugging his knees. In spite of his determination not to cry, his lower lip *would* keep trembling, and there was a twitch under his right eye that he could not control. *Mother—not coming home?* Ezra couldn't believe it. He rubbed his nose and reached up to straighten his leather headband.

Tola sat opposite him on a short three-legged stool, making no attempt to conceal his tears. "She says she doesn't belong here anymore. She's found someone who . . . *understands* her better . . . or believes as she does. More *open-minded*. Like King Ahaz. At least that's the message I got."

King Ahaz. Ezra would never again be able to think of King Ahaz in quite the same way. Banished forever was the image of the engaging, confident, persuasive leader of men. In its place was a picture of a shrunken, careworn, frightened child in an adult body, racked with anxiety and indecision, cowering before the horrible demands of the Red King.

"But Father, don't you even know where to find her?"

Tola raised an eyebrow and gave his son a piercing look. "I was hoping *you* might have an idea," he said significantly.

Ezra's face burned with shame. He bowed his head. "I'm sorry, Father," he said. "I told you she wasn't there. I saw Hanun, but not Mother. Not once. I looked for her—I looked hard! But it was dark, and the light of the flames distorted everything, and most of the women had their faces covered."

He paused. His vision blurred. Into his mind came a picture of the narrow alley off Mishneh Street, all striped awnings, dirty and tattered, blowing in the night breeze, with grotesque faces leering at him in the half-light cast by oil lamps and charcoal braziers. He saw baubled and bangled women stretching out their hands to him from shadowy nooks and stone archways. Again, in his imagination, he stared up at the Tower of Ophel and gaped open-mouthed at the high place, the altar, and the forest of Asherah poles, bright with little fluttering banners. A sudden idea struck him.

"Father," he said, "I *might* know where to find her. I really might! Can I go out and look?"

"We've been over this," his father said sternly. "You're confined to this house for the next two weeks. No—make that a month! Do you understand me, young man? After last night's little escapade I've a good mind to put an iron ring in the wall and tie you to it like a donkey. You simply have no idea, Ezra. No idea. Why, for a while there I thought I'd lost *both* of you!" He paused, and for a brief moment the ruddy, bearded face flushed red. "I suppose you'll never know until you have children of your own."

"I said I was sorry, Father," said Ezra, squeezing his eyes shut and pressing them against his knees until he saw stars. "You have no idea how sorry I really am!"

Then the tears came, and he made no further attempt to hold them back. Why had he never realized before how much his father cared about him and his mother? He knew now that he was something much more to him than a prophetic sign or wonder. He knew—and felt—that Tola, like Isaiah, was a man possessed—possessed by love. A man who would sooner die than buy peace or prosperity or personal achievement by sacrificing his own son. Why couldn't he have recognized it sooner?

Tola got to his feet, wiping his face with the back of one hand. Then he reached down and ran his fingers through his son's tangled black locks. "Do you know what?" he said. "I believe you this time. Somehow or other, I believe you really *are* sorry. But we don't have time to mope about our troubles now. There's another meeting of the Remnant tonight. We'd better have some supper before the prophet and the others arrive. Looks like lots more stale loaves and sour *leben* for you and me. At least until Old Hephzibah's arm heals up. Oh, didn't I tell you? She's promised to stay and cook for us. For a while, anyway. Until your mother . . . changes her mind." Ezra looked up and saw him smile sadly as he turned to leave the room.

By the time the members of the Remnant began to gather, Ezra was feeling more like himself again. *Maybe more like a new self*, he thought as he watched them file through the door.

First came the slight young Elisabeth, one of the king's kitchen maids, who blushed and smiled when Ezra caught her eye, then hurried in to sit beside Old Hephzibah. She was followed by Ira, the hunchbacked weaver, and Ben-Shimri, a hard-fisted, square-jawed silversmith who had lost most of his business because of his refusal to make images of the Baals and Asherahs. Acsah, the round-faced wife of Ezra's tutor, Mishael, was there too, and Maacah the baker's daughter, and Pua, who served as a reserve member of the King's Guard. They weren't the kind of people Ezra would have chosen as friends—not most of them, anyway. In the past, he would have laughed at them and called them "losers" and "a bunch of nobodies." But tonight he seemed to see them with new eyes. Tonight they felt like family. Somehow, in his mind, they glowed with a soft, warm light that was altogether different from the lurid, leaping glow of the flames in the idol's belly. *Signs and wonders in Israel* were the words that popped into his head as members of the group passed him and went to find a place to sit on the floor of the main room.

Finally the prophet himself entered—tall, stern-eyed, his dark brow furrowed with lines that reminded Ezra of the creases in his own father's forehead. He was followed by his wife, the lively little Abigail, who flitted through the door on tip-toe and directed a few soft-spoken but intense words at Ezra's father before moving on into the interior of the house. Trailing after her came fuzzy-haired, red-cheeked Maher-Shalal-Hash-Baz. He raised an eyebrow at Ezra and gave him a knowing smirk before sweeping past on the hem of his mother's skirts. Any other time Ezra would have felt like bashing him in the face. Tonight he just shook his head.

Last of all came a face Ezra hadn't expected to see. "Shub!" he said. "What are *you* doing here?"

Shub looked sheepish. He put a finger to his lips and shuffled his big feet. "I had to come," he said. "After last night, I . . . well, it's just that everything has . . . *changed* somehow."

Ezra nodded but said nothing.

"Besides," Shub went on, "without my harp I don't have anything to do at home. My father says the only way I'll ever get another *kinnor* is if I build it myself or earn the money to buy one . . . and neither one of those is easy." He bit his lip and frowned. "He's *really* mad, Ezra."

Ezra frowned, too, and nodded again.

"But mostly I came to talk to *you*. I keep thinking about last night. It still seems like some kind of weird dream. I keep remembering the things you said. Did you mean it?"

Ezra blushed and stared down at his feet. "Mean what?"

"You know. What you said to that priest in the big red robe and all those other people. About abominations and consequences and Yahweh, God of Israel. You were like . . . like some kind of *hero*, Ezra! Like Moses or Joshua or Elijah. I couldn't believe it! Did you mean it? Or was it just another one of your tricks?"

Ezra looked his friend in the face. "I'm not sure if I meant it *then*," he said slowly. "But—" and at this he glanced in at the plain, humble faces of the people who were sitting on the floor of his father's house, talking in low voices, waiting for the prophet to start the meeting, "I think I do *now*. I was wrong, Shub. Something bad *did* happen. And it would have been worse," he shuddered, "much worse, except that—I don't know—except that God, the *real* God, really *was* watching out for Hezekiah. Just like your father said He would. I was wrong, and Hezekiah was right. I should have known all along. I guess I'm just too stubborn."

"Well, I'm glad to hear you say so," said a voice at the door. Ezra and Shub wheeled around at the sound. There, draped in the same soiled and torn street-urchin's cloak that he had worn to the pagan high places on the two previous nights, stood the stocky little prince, breathing hard, his round, ruddy face glistening with sweat.

"I came to join the Remnant," said Hezekiah in answer to their blank stares. "Had to sneak out to do it, too. Ran all the way here. You taught me well, Ezra," he added with a grin. "Not that it was all that hard. My father has been trying to avoid me all day."

From the inner room came the deep, melodic voice of the prophet, who had risen at last to address the gathering of the Remnant. "Comfort, comfort my people, says your God," he chanted in slow and soothing tones.

> Speak tenderly to Jerusalem, and proclaim
> to her
> That her hard service has been completed,
> That her sin has been paid for,
> That she has received from the Lord's hand
> double for all her sins.

Ezra straightened his leather headband and smiled. Then he grabbed Hezekiah by the hand and pulled him into the house.

"Come on," he said. "We'll *all* join! And I've got a feeling that it'll be the biggest and best adventure we've ever had. *You'll* see!"

Letters From Our Readers

This story is scary, especially the part about Molech worship and the strange parties the idol worshipers had.

Brent Parsons, Indianapolis, IN

Idol worship *is* scary! The boys shouldn't have gone to the high places at all. Sometimes, like Ezra, we think that we can get away with doing things we know are wrong. But there are consequences to dabbling in evil. Ezra found that out when his friend Hezekiah was almost sacrificed to the evil god Molech.

Unfortunately, people aren't very different today. They start out doing things they think are "innocent," such as reading horoscopes, playing with Ouija boards, or listening to phone psychics. Once they get caught up in the occult, though, it's easy to get deeper and deeper into it until they're hooked, just like the Molech worshipers. The Bible tells us to stay strictly away from idols and evil practices (see Deuteronomy 18:10–12; 1 Corinthians 10:14, 10:20–21; Galatians 5:19–21).

Where can I find this story in the Bible, anyway?

Josh Reinhardt, Cheyenne, WY

You'll find the basis for this story in the Book of Isaiah, 2 Chronicles 28, and 2 Kings 16, all in the Old Testament. Isaiah was a prophet who wrote during the reigns of King Ahaz and King Hezekiah, when the Assyrian Empire was expanding into Canaan. Isaiah warned the people about worshiping the Assyrian gods, which didn't make him very popular. Isaiah had at least two sons, Shear-Jashub (Isaiah 7:3) and Maher-Shalal-Hash-Baz (Isaiah 8:3).

You won't find any mention of Ezra or his dad, Tola, in the Bible, though. We imagined what it would be like to be a prophet's kid. What if this boy got tired of everyone expecting him to be super good, like his father and the prophet Isaiah? What if he was just a bit too curious and wanted to find out if all those stories about idol worship were true? What if he thought nothing bad could happen to him? Maybe you know someone like that.

Did King Ahaz really sacrifice his children to a false god?

Danielle Montgomery, Greenville, SC

We're afraid so. The Bible says, "He walked in the ways of the kings of Israel and also made cast idols for worshiping the Baals. He burned sacrifices in the Valley of Ben Hinnom and sacrificed his sons in the fire, following the detestable ways of the nations the Lord had driven out before the Israelites" (2 Chronicles 28:2–3).

The boys mentioned the prophecy that says, "For to us a child is born, to us a son is given..." They said it was about Hezekiah, but I thought that prophecy was about Jesus.

Justin Mendenhall, Chicago, IL

Many interpreters of Scripture think that Isaiah's immediate thoughts were focused on present-day events when he uttered those words, that he really was hoping and expecting that Ahaz's son would turn around the sad state of affairs that had developed under Ahaz. Many centuries later, we can look back and see that his words had a much larger meaning—a reference point that he himself was perhaps unaware of. Much of Old Testament prophecy is like that. For example, God tells David that his "son" will "build a house" to the Lord's name, and that his throne or dynasty will never end. The obvious immediate reference is to Solomon and the temple. But in the long run, Solomon turned out to be a big disappointment, the temple was destroyed, Judah ceased to be a nation, and the line of her kings failed. So the prophecy must have some larger reference—to Jesus and the "house" that He would build in the form of His church.

Did Bible-era kids really talk back to their parents the way Ezra did in this story? My parents wouldn't let me do that, and I don't even live in Bible times.

Matthew Martinez, Anchorage, AK

Since no one can say exactly how kids acted and spoke back in Bible times, authors have to use their imaginations and what they know about the culture to guess at what life might have been like. Kids tend to be the same in any time period, so maybe they forgot sometimes, just like you do, and talked back to their parents. No matter what culture or era we live in, though, God wants us to respect our parents and others. (See Leviticus 19:3; 1 Peter 2:17.)

It seems like many of the kings of Israel and Judah worshiped false gods. How about Hezekiah? What happened when he grew up?

Kyle Hendricks, Toledo, OH

He's called "good King Hezekiah" for a reason. In 2 Kings 18:5-6, it says, "Hezekiah trusted in the Lord, the God of Israel. There was no one like him among all the kings of Judah, either before him or after him. He held fast to the Lord and did not cease to follow him; he kept the commands the Lord had given Moses." It also says that he removed the high places and the Asherah poles and broke up the sacred stones and the bronze snake Moses had made. You can read the story of Hezekiah's reign in 2 Kings 18-20 and 2 Chronicles 29-32.